Irish Tales

Irish TALES:

O R,

Instructive HISTORIES for the happy Conduct of LIFE.

Containing the following Events.

VIZ.

I. The Captivated MONARCH.
II. The Banish'd PRINCE.
III. The Power of BEAUTY.
IV. The Distrest LOVERS.
V. The Perfidious GALLANT.
VI. The Constant FAIR-ONE.
VII. The Generous RIVAL.
VIII The Inhuman FATHER.
IX. The Depos'd USURPER.
X. The Punishment of UNGENEROUS LOVE.

By Mrs. SARAH BUTLER.

LONDON: Printed for *E. Curll* at the *Dial* and *Bible*, and *J. Hooke*, at the *Flower-de-Luce*, both against St. *Dunstan*'s Church in *Fleetstreet*, 1716.
Price 1 *s.* 6 *d.* Stitch'd, 2 *s.* Bound.

IRISH TALES:
OR,
INSTRUCTIVE HISTORIES FOR THE HAPPY CONDUCT OF LIFE

Sarah Butler

edited with an introduction and notes by
Ian Campbell Ross, Aileen Douglas and Anne Markey

FOUR COURTS PRESS

Set in 10.5 pt on 13 pt Bembo for
FOUR COURTS PRESS LTD
7 Malpas Street, Dublin 8, Ireland
www.fourcourtspress.ie
and in North America for
FOUR COURTS PRESS
c/o ISBS, 920 N.E. 58th Avenue, Suite 300, Portland, OR 97213.

A catalogue record for this title
is available from the British Library.

ISBN 978-1-84682-216-2 hbk
978-1-84682-217-9 pbk

Printed in England
by Antony Rowe Ltd, Chippenham, Wilts.

Contents

The Literature of Early Modern Ireland series

Titles in the series:
Faithful Teate, *Ter Tria*, ed. Angelina Lynch (2007)
Henry Burkhead, *Cola's Furie*, ed. Angelina Lynch and Patricia Coughlan (2009)
Richard Nugent, *Cynthia*, ed. Angelina Lynch and Anne Fogarty (2010)
William Dunkin, *The Parson's Revels*, ed. Catherine Skeen (2010)

Early Irish Fiction, *c.*1680–1820

Also published in the series:
[Anon.], *Vertue Rewarded; or, The Irish Princess* (1693), ed. Ian Campbell Ross and Anne Markey

Forthcoming titles in the series:
Thomas Amory, *The Life of John Buncle, Esq.* (1756), ed. Moyra Haslett
Henry Brooke, *Juliet Grenville; or, the history of the human heart* (1774), ed. Sandro Jung

Preface

Irish prose fiction of the long eighteenth century has only recently begun to receive the attention it merits. While such names as Swift, Goldsmith and Edgeworth have long been familiar to readers of Irish (and British) literature, many other writers – born, educated, or living in Ireland – produced a substantial and imaginatively varied body of fiction from the late-seventeenth to the early-nineteenth century. This series aims more fully to indicate the diversity and breadth of Irish literature in the period 1680–1820 by providing critical editions of a range of exemplary works of prose fiction. In so doing, it will indicate the role the early novel played in inventing Ireland for readers at home and abroad, while offering new perspectives on the literature and history of these islands.

Each title in the series will contain a carefully-edited text, together with a critical introduction, a select bibliography, and comprehensive notes, designed for scholars and students of Irish writing in English, of the English novel, and all those concerned with Ireland *c.*1680–*c.*1820.

Aileen Douglas
Moyra Haslett
Ian Campbell Ross
January 2010

Acknowledgments

The editors gratefully acknowledge the award by the Irish Research Council for the Humanities and Social Sciences of a Small Research Grant (2008–10) for Early Irish Fiction, *c.*1680–*c.*1820. We also gratefully acknowledge financial assistance from the Long Room Hub, Trinity College Dublin, and the Centre for Irish-Scottish and Comparative Studies, Trinity College Dublin.

For their generosity in answering queries, the editors are grateful to Bernadette Cunningham, Seán Duffy, Jill Gage, Moyra Haslett, Benjamin Hazard, JoEllen McKillop Dickie, G. Martin Murphy, and Muireann Ní Bhrolcháin.

The frontispiece illustration of the title-page of the first edition of *Irish Tales* (1716) is reproduced by permission of the Board of Trinity College Dublin.

Introduction

'Lasting and Terrible were the bloody Wars which the Ancient *Irish* sustain'd against the powerful *Danes*'.[1] The dramatic opening words of Sarah Butler's *Irish Tales* introduced readers to a genuinely new fictional subject. While early-eighteenth century readers would, by the conclusion of the novel, have recognized it as a fiction centering on the clash between public duty and private desire – a characteristic theme in a great deal of early fiction in English – aspects of the work would still have been completely unexpected and decidedly unfamiliar. Today, the work's full title, *Irish Tales: or, Instructive Histories for the Happy Conduct of Life* is likely to strike readers as bland or, still worse, off-putting. In 1716, however, that same title might have caught the eye of readers for quite different reasons. Few works of contemporary fiction were 'Irish' and those that were rarely suggested themselves as models for the 'happy conduct of life'.[2] In fact, Sarah Butler's only known work contains a great deal that is quite distinctive, both in the author's subject matter and her treatment of it, setting *Irish Tales* apart from the general run of 'tales', 'novels', and 'romances' whose rapidly growing popularity was so remarkable a feature of contemporary literature.

Today, readers will quickly recognize the power of a familiar episode of Irish history, relating the Gaelic Irish resistance to Viking invasions from the ninth to the eleventh centuries, that culminated with victory under Brian Boru at the battle of Clontarf on Good Friday 1014. Since the battle is characterized as having given 'the last total Defeat to the Danes' in Ireland, such readers will easily see the allegorical possibilities of the historical narrative Sarah Butler presented to her contemporaries. *Irish Tales* was published just a quarter of a cen-

1 Sarah Butler, *Irish Tales: or, Instructive Histories for the Happy Conduct of Life* (London, 1716), p. 1; all subsequent references will be to the present edition and given parenthetically in the text.

2 Works of fiction with 'Irish' in the title published over the previous quarter of a century are restricted to the anonymous *The Irish Rogue; or, The comical history of the life and actions of Teague O'Divelley, from his birth to the present year, 1690* (London [1690]), *The Wild-Irish Captain, or Villany display'd truly and faithfully related* (London, 1692), and *Vertue Rewarded; or, The Irish Princess* (1693), of which the last is unique in offering a positively inflected account of Ireland. Verse titles were scarcely more encouraging, including as they did *The New Irish Christmass Box; or, The Female Dear Joy trick'd out of her Maiden Head. To an excellent new Teagueland Tune* (London? [[n.d.] *c.*1700?) or *The Irish Hieroglyphick; or, A dialogue between a reverend rattlesnake, and a Dublin swan* (Dublin, 1710).

tury after the 1691 Treaty of Limerick left the protestant William III and his army, famously containing several thousand Danish mercenaries, victorious in his struggle against the catholic James II. Equally strikingly, the fiction appeared within months of the Jacobite Rebellion of 1715, which had sought to place James's son, the Old Pretender, on the thrones of Great Britain and Ireland. Only a careful reading of Sarah Butler's novel, however, will reveal the full extent of the author's ingenuity in the deployment of her major historical sources, despite her clear insistence that the work is indeed founded on history. And what a casual modern reading of *Irish Tales* obscures is how remarkable a work it was for its time: as parallel history; in the imaginative handling of its source materials; the bold construction of the narrative; its complex interrogation of the conduct demanded of individuals when public duty and private desire conflict; and its articulation of hopes for the future success of the Jacobite cause in Ireland.

It was in London that *Irish Tales* first appeared, in 1716. The bookseller at whose shop it was to be found was a notoriously unscrupulous figure in the English capital in the early decades of the eighteenth century, whose wares included works by notable writers including Jonathan Swift and Alexander Pope, but works not always published with their authors' permission.[3] Nor, it would seem, were Curll's customers necessarily more scrupulous than the bookseller himself; a later Irish novelist Thomas Amory wrote of Curll that he was 'intimate with all the high whores in town', adding that 'many of them frequented his shop, to buy his dialogues, and other lively books'.[4] As Curll also published poetry, some novels, political writings, and important antiquarian texts, it is certain that many other, more respectable customers frequented his shop at the sign of the Dial and Bible in Fleet Street. But the customer inspecting the latest publications was doubtless aware of Curll's dubious reputation as she – for the prospective purchaser of a new novel would most likely have been

3 Curll published Swift's *Meditations on a Broomstick* (1710) and a volume of *Miscellanies* (1711), as well as his own *A Complete Key to The Tale of a Tub; with some account of the authors, the occasion and design of writing it, and Mr. Wotton's Remarks Examin'd* (1710). In these same years, he also published two more sensational works with Irish connections: Nicholas Bernard's *The Case of John Atherton, Bishop of Waterford in Ireland; who was convicted for the sin of uncleanness with a cow, and other creatures* (1710), and *Some Memorials of the Life and Penitent Death of Dr. John Atherton, Bishop of Waterford in Ireland; who was executed at Dublin, Dec. 5, 1640* (1711). In 1716, the same year that saw the appearance of *Irish Tales*, Curll also published an unauthorized edition of three town eclogues, two by Lady Mary Wortley Montagu and one by John Gay, under the title *Court Poems*, as a result of which Alexander Pope first tricked Curll into drinking a powerful emetic and subsequently published a pamphlet entitled *A Full and True Account of a Horrid and Barbarous Revenge by Poison, on the Body of Mr. Edmund Curll, Bookseller* (1716) followed, a few days later, by *A Further Account of the Most Deplorable Condition of Mr. Edmund Curll, Bookseller* (1716).

4 Thomas Amory, *The Life of John Buncle, Esq.* 2 vols (London, 1766), ii, p. 384.

female – leafed through the opening pages of *Irish Tales*. If what she found was not quite what Amory would have called a 'lively book' then it was certainly intriguing.

Irish Tales opens with a dedicatory epistle and a preface. While the preface was the author's, the dedicatory epistle indicated that the author, Mrs Sarah Butler, was dead. This epistle was the work of the miscellaneous writer and controversialist, Charles Gildon, obsequiously addressed, as were many such dedications, to a nobleman. The authorial preface was far less predictable in content. Many contemporary prefaces teased out, as did this one, possible relationships between the truth of history and the forms of fiction. Here, however, was no generic or generalized consideration of these vexed issues but rather a precise, detailed, and impassioned discussion of the rare, in some cases extremely rare, historical sources for the author's story. The nature of that story, involving resistance by the Irish to successive waves of northern invaders, was also surprising.

It was not that bloody Wars were in themselves unknown as the subject matter for popular literature. If Homer's *Iliad* remained a widely read work among educated readers, whether in the original Greek, in Latin translations studied at school, or in English versions such as that the age's leading poet, Alexander Pope, had begun to publish in 1715, then those who preferred prose might enjoy famous episodes from the siege of Troy related in the anonymously-authored *Trojan Tales* (1714), which promised stories told by Ulysses, Helenus, Hector, Achilles, and Priam. What distinguished Butler's account of warfare was the author's recourse to the centuries long struggle between the 'Ancient *Irish*' and the 'powerful *Danes*'. In 1716, the revival of interest in the middle ages that would characterize a great deal of later-eighteenth century poetry and prose, from James Thomson through Horace Walpole, James Macpherson or Ann Radcliffe, to William Blake, had hardly begun. Indeed, it is doubtful that the generality of readers could even have dated the wars between the Irish and Danish, or Viking, invaders with any precision, for most of the sources for history then so obscure were in long-out-of-print volumes or hidden in scholarly tomes, such as Camden's *Britannia* (1586; 7th ed. 1607; trans. into English by Philémon Holland, 1610). For most historians – even Irish historians writing in English, such as Richard Cox, author of *Hibernia Anglicana; or, the History of Ireland from the Conquest there by the English to this present time* (1689–90) – Ireland entered history only when the Norman invaders left England during the reign of Henry II in order to subject the neighbouring island. When Ireland did enter history, it was generally to create problems for the English, so that one account of the country, published in the wake of the victory of the protestant William III over the catholic James II, opened with the words:

> The Kingdom of *Ireland*, has for several Ages been an Aceldama, or Field of Slaughter, watered with the Blood of *English* Men; occasioned by their Repeated Rebellions, and inveterate aversion to the *English* Nation, in

> pursuance whereof, they have left no Treacheries, Murders, or Villanies unattempted, being incouraged thereto by their Ignorant and Superstitious Priests, to whose Dictates, this Stupid People entirely submit, and who endeavour to Foment and Cherish this Inexorable hatred, formerly under pretence of recovering their Liberty ...[5]

Even if this was an extreme view, the idea that tales of Ireland, especially an Ireland whose history was for most readers shrouded in darkness, might – as Butler's title promised – provide 'Instructive histories for the happy Conduct of Life' seemed improbable in the extreme.

The prolific and varied output of Edmund Curll, publisher of *Irish Tales*, did however contain some unexpected items, not least numerous works with Jacobite leanings. In April 1716, for instance, Curll published *An Account of the Tryal of the Earl of Winton*. Wintoun was the only leading figure tried for involvement in the 1715 Jacobite rebellion to plead not guilty; convicted after a protracted trial that whetted public interest in the case, he was awaiting execution in the Tower of London in April (though he escaped in August, allegedly by filing through the bars of his cell with a watch spring).[6] While novels did not form a large part of Curll's publishing output, one novelist he did publish was herself a well-known Jacobite. This was Jane Barker, whose *Love's Intrigues* had appeared in 1713. The full title, *Love's Intrigues: or, the History of the Amours of Bosvil and Galesia, as related to Lucasia, in St. Germains Garden*, contains the clue to the novel's political leanings, for Jane Barker had followed James II into exile in France, joining his court at St Germain-en-Laye. In 1714, Curll published Barker's *Exilius; or the Banish'd Roman: a new Romance*, a work that readers could easily interpret as both allegorical and Jacobite.[7] Curll continued to publish Barker's work until 1724.

In such a context, the very name of the author of *Irish Tales* was, as one writer has recently noted, undoubtedly 'resonant'.[8] Of Sarah Butler, the reader is told simply in the opening line of the dedication that 'The Fair Authress of the

5 R.B., 'To the Reader', *The History of the Kingdom of Ireland* (London, 1693), p. [v].

6 John L. Roberts, *The Jacobite Wars: Scotland and the Military Campaigns of 1715 and 1745* (Edinburgh: Polygon, 2002), pp 35–7. The official order for publishing the proceedings had been given to Jacob Tonson, but the cost of this version being found prohibitive, Curll produced a significantly cheaper version, priced at only 2*d*., but was arrested and held in custody until 11 May, only being released because he went on his knees before the Lord Chamberlain who reprimanded him severely; William Roberts, *The Earlier History of English Bookselling* (London: S. Lowe, Marston, Searle, & Rivington, 1889), pp 235–6.

7 See Kathryn R. King, *Jane Barker, Exile; A Literary Career, 1675–1725* (Oxford: Clarendon Press, 2000), pp 152–4; *Exilius* bears the date 1715 on its title-page but was in fact published in August 1714.

8 See Toby Barnard, *Improving Ireland? Projectors, Prophets, and Profiteers* (Dublin: Four Courts Press, 2008), p. 103.

following sheets [is] dead' (p. 35), and will learn no more of her. The most famous Butler in 1716, however, was another Jacobite, James Butler, second duke of Ormond (1665–1745). Irish born, and a distinguished military commander under William III and Queen Anne, Ormond became Lord-Lieutenant of Ireland in 1703 but lost the post a decade later, shortly before he began regular contact with the Jacobite court in France. In 1714 he went into exile and in the following year was appointed captain-general of the Jacobite forces at the time of the 1715 Rebellion, joining the court in exile at Avignon after the rebellion's suppression. A novel entitled *Irish Tales* written by an author named Butler, and published by Edmund Curll, could hardly have avoided arousing suspicions that its sympathies might be Jacobite.[9] The name of the author and the bald assertion that she was dead would have intrigued the contemporary browser and must prompt the modern reader to wonder whether Sarah Butler existed at all, or was a convenient fiction.[10]

If Sarah Butler did not exist, however, the question of the authorship of *Irish Tales* remains vexed. Charles Gildon himself has been suggested as the author, though the suggestion is based on no particular evidence.[11] But if Gildon was not

9 James Butler, duke of Ormond, was so celebrated a figure in his age that almost half a century later, the Irish-born Laurence Sterne gave his name to Uncle Toby's servant, known as Corporal Trim (*recte* James Butler), in *Tristram Shandy* (1759–67), making great play of the coincidence of names (II, v; IV, xviii); see *The Life and Opinions of Tristram Shandy, Gentleman*, ed. Ian Campbell Ross (1983; new ed. Oxford: Oxford University Press, 2009), pp 76–7, 234–5.

10 Attempts to identify Sarah Butler have failed. There appear to have been no Butlers with that given name in the late-seventeenth century. The anonymous *Some Account of the Family of the Butlers, but more particularly of the late Duke of* Ormond, *the Earl of* Ossory *his Father, and James, Duke of* Ormond *his Grandfather* (London, 1716), for instance, records the earl of Ossory (d. 1680) as having had six daughters: Elizabeth, Amelia, Henrietta, Catherine, Mary, and Henrietta; see Ian Campbell Ross, '"One of the Principal Nations in Europe": The Representation of Ireland in Sarah Butler's *Irish Tales*', *Eighteenth-Century Fiction*, 7:1 (1994), 1–16 (7 n. 13). For an unconvincing attempt to identify the author of *Irish Tales* with the widow of a Williamite officer killed at the battle of Aughrim in 1691, see J.T. Leerssen, 'On the Treatment of Irishness in Romantic Anglo-Irish Fiction', *Irish University Review*, 20:2 (1990), 251–63 (252).

11 Both Kathryn R. King, *Jane Barker*, p. 174 and Toby Barnard, *Improving Ireland?* , p. 103 doubt the existence of Sarah Butler. For suggestions that Gildon may have written *Irish Tales*, see W.H. McBurney, *A Check List of English Prose Fiction, 1700–1739* (Cambridge: Harvard University Press, 1960), p. 36 and Germaine Greer, 'Women in the Literary Market Place', in Sarah Prescott and David E. Shuttleton (eds), *Women and Poetry, 1660–1750* (Basingstoke: Palgrave Macmillan, 2003), p. 176. In politics, Gildon leaned towards the Whigs and there is no evidence he had Jacobite sympathies, or an interest in Ireland. The sentiments he expresses in the 'Epistle Dedicatory', however, are certainly a reworking of similar ideas about arms and arts advanced in the 'Epistle Dedicatory' to *The Patriot* (1703), adapted from Nathaniel Lee's tragedy, *Lucius Junius Brutus* (1680), whose dramatic situations and vocabulary both find occasional echoes in *Irish Tales*.

the author, then where did he get the 'sheets' he brought to publication? Relegating speculation to a footnote, it is perhaps best to accept the contemporary attribution of the authorship of *Irish Tales* to Sarah Butler, accepting this shadowy figure as an Irish woman of considerable intelligence and Jacobite leanings, having access to a library containing historical materials as little known as they are important.[12]

If the writing of *Irish Tales* suggests an author close to highly literate circles, the book itself was indisputably a luxury item. *Irish Tales* cost 1*s*. 6*d*. 'stitched' or 2*s* 'bound': no small amount for any but well-to-do readers in an age when a male labourer could hope for 1*s*. 4*d*. a day, a female servant's wage might be as low as £3 a year (plus board), while a charity school mistress would have to make do with what she could save from the £60 a year allotted for the rent of premises, heating, books, and clothing for her pupils, besides her own salary.[13] The title-page that *Irish Tales* presented to its purchasers insinuated them into a literary version of elite culture by playing knowingly with the conventions of heroic romance, to the extent of numbering and entitling the 'tales':

I. The Captivated MONARCH.

II. The Banish'd PRINCE.

III. The Power of BEAUTY.

IV. The Distrest LOVERS

and so on, down to 'X. The Punishment of UNGENEROUS LOVE'. While the invitation to a Jacobite reading of the novel is encouraged by these titles, any

12 Among names that suggest themselves as possible authors of *Irish Tales* one is especially intriguing. This is Capt. John Stevens, an English Roman Catholic Jacobite who had fought for James II in Ireland in 1689–91 and who, after a period of exile, had returned to England in the mid-1690s to lead the life of a miscellaneous writer. Stevens's varied works included a translation of *Don Quixote*, collected translations of travel writings, an English-Spanish dictionary, and eventually a version of Louis Alemand's *Histoire Monastique d'Irlande* (1690), published as *Monasticon Hibernicum; or, the Monastical History of Ireland* (1722), in the preface of which Stevens articulates a view of pre-Norman Ireland, the 'island of saints and scholars' not dissimilar to that put forward in *Irish Tales*. John Stevens succeeded Charles Gildon as editor of *The British Mercury* in 1712. For accounts of Stevens, see Martin Murphy, 'A Jacobite Antiquary in Grub Street: Capt. John Stevens (*c*.1662–1726)', *Recusant History*, 24:4 (1999), 437–54, and the same author's entry on Stevens in the *Oxford Dictionary of National Biography*. For the privileged access to specialized printed and manuscript materials on the part of the author of *Irish Tales*, see below, pp 17–20.

13 Bernard Mandeville, *The Fable of the Bees; or Private Vices, Publick Benefits. With an Essay on Charity and Charity Schools* (London, 1724), p. 344; Daniel Defoe, *Every-body's Business, is Nobody's Business; or, Private Abuses, Publick Grievances, exemplified in the Pride, Insolence, and Exorbitant Wages of our Women-Servants, Footmen &c* (London, 1725), p. 5; *An Account of Charity-Schools in Great Britain and Ireland; with the benefactions thereto, and the Methods by which they were set up, and are governed* (11th ed. London, 1712), p. 9.

female customer in Curll's shop – whatever her political views – would have recognized *Irish Tales* as a fiction invoking the conventions of heroic romance. Indeed, so stylized a presentation of the work allowed for the possibility that its historical foundation might, like that of many contemporary fictions, be little more than an exotic backdrop to the story of high-born characters, torn between the competing demands of private and public life, of love and duty. Since the unfortunate loves of the princess Dooneflaith and the prince Murchoe form the dominant narrative thread of *Irish Tales*, an understanding of Butler's work as a series of short heroic romances might be thought appropriate enough. The title, and title-page, of Sarah Butler's work are, however, doubly misleading. Despite the listing of ten separate 'tales', the fiction that follows is a through-composed narrative and while it is possible to identify the episodes mentioned they are not so identified in any way in the text itself, making *Irish Tales* formally quite different to *Trojan Tales*, for instance. Conversely, the construction of *Irish Tales* as a continuous narrative distinguishes it also from, say, Jane Barker's *Exilius* which, though described on its title-page as a 'new romance', is in fact composed of a series of separate but intersecting tales, such as 'The History of Clelia' or 'The History of Clarinthia', related (mostly) by the protagonists to a small audience, of which 'The History of Exilius' is only one.

Despite the evidence of Butler's narrative itself, Charles Gildon nevertheless appears to have understood the work whose publication he had undertaken – but had perhaps not read carefully – as a collection of tales. In his 'Epistle Dedicatory', he alluded to the success of those 'Books of TALES' that follow the model of the *Milesian Tales* (p. 37). In line with the quest for classical precedent that characterized a great deal of contemporary literature, Gildon here refers to the collection of works written by the Greek author of the second century BC, Aristides of Miletus, from whose birthplace the name 'Milesian' derived. Despite Gildon's reference to 'so many Books of Tales', late-seventeenth and early-eighteenth century English literature did not, to the modern eye, boast many examples of such works. Thomas d'Urfey's *Tales tragical and comical* (1704) was a compendium of short tales in both prose and verse, translated from French, Italian and Spanish. Most volumes published under the title 'Tales' were in fact translations: from Boccaccio's celebrated and much reprinted *Decameron* (the model followed by Barker in *Exilius*), *Persian and Turkish Tales* (1714), *The Thousand and One Nights* or, in Ambrose Philips's rendering, *The Thousand and One Days* (1714–5), Thomas-Simon Gueullette's *Tartarian Tales* (1716), or the fairy tales written by Madame d'Aulnoy, which appeared in English translation from 1699, reaching their final form in *The History of the Tales of the Fairies* (1716). In such circumstances, the title *Irish Tales* carried with it decidedly exotic connotations. Rightly so perhaps for, in the strict dictionary definition of 'exotic' as 'belonging to another country, foreign, alien', this was exactly what *Irish Tales* was.

By 1716, Charles Gildon, the writer who introduced *Irish Tales* to the world, had a colourful publishing history behind him. At one time a notorious deist, who dared to defend suicide against all religious prohibitions, and who wrote a history of deism, he had latterly renounced such heterodox beliefs in favour of adherence to the Church of England.[14] Gildon's work included plays, fiction and literary criticism, and he was briefly editor of the *British Mercury*, in which role he enjoyed no better success than with his other literary endeavours, while managing to quarrel with both Jonathan Swift and Alexander Pope. Most pertinently, given his relationship to Butler's work, Gildon had earlier produced a collection of the novels of Aphra Behn, under the title *All the Histories and Novels written by the late ingenious Mrs. Behn*, to which he added a preface in which he compared the force of Behn's imagination to Homer's.[15] By 1716, Charles Gildon was little more than a hack-writer. The dedicatee of *Irish Tales*, by contrast, was a man of some eminence: Henry Clinton, seventh earl of Lincoln, who the previous year, at the age of thirty-one, had served as Paymaster-General of the army during the Jacobite rebellion. As ever, Gildon was on the look-out for a patron but while the flattery he bestows on the earl might, like that of most dedications, be taken guardedly, the ways in which he represents the book he has prepared for the press are revealing.

As Gildon suggests, *Irish Tales* concerns 'HEROIC LOVE, and all the PATRIOT VIRTUES' (p. 35). What is less expected is that Gildon does not simply assert that such qualities will find protection under Lincoln but links them directly to the earl's recent service as Paymaster-General of the British army during the recent Jacobite rebellion. When that rebellion broke out in the late summer of 1715, it was thought that Ireland, with an overwhelmingly large Roman Catholic population that had seen the bulk of its lands confiscated over the past three-quarters of a century, would be a focus of Jacobite defiance towards the new Hanoverian monarchy. In the event, and despite the duke of Ormond's role as captain-general of the Jacobite forces, the country remained quiet and the rebellion was largely confined to Scotland, and to the north and west of England.[16] Even if 'patriot virtues' are understood, in line with contemporary values, as principled loyalty to king and parliament in defence of national

14 Charles Gildon edited the writings of the deist Charles Blount as *The Miscellaneous Works of Charles Blount, Esq* (1695), and added his own deistical thoughts in *The Oracles of Reason* (1693), before recanting in *The Deist's Manual* (1705).

15 'So that this Reflection ought to raise our Admiration of Mrs. Behn, whose Genius was of that Force like *Homer*'s, to maintain its Gayety in the midst of Disappointments, which a Woman of her Sense and Merit, ought never to have met with'; *All the Histories and Novels written by the late ingenious Mrs. Behn* (4th ed. 1700), 'The Epistle Dedicatory', [n.p.]. There is considerable doubt as to whether all the novels Gildon published as Behn's were in fact by her; see, for example, Greer, 'Women in the Literary Market Place', pp 171–2 and Jane Spencer, *Aphra Behn's Afterlife* (Oxford: Oxford University Press, 2000), pp 125–7.

16 The duke of Ormond in fact remained in France throughout the rebellion.

independence, the association of Lincoln with a book that roundly asserts the rights of Ireland to self-determination, from a Jacobite standpoint, is indubitably strange. Much of Gildon's dedication in fact suggests a mixture of commonplace ideas about the connection between martial glory and the arts in classical antiquity, an unthinking allegiance to ascendent Whig political values, and a striking inability to read Butler's narrative in terms of the Irish and catholic national and religious values it undoubtedly embodies.

Sarah Butler's preface, meanwhile, like the novel itself, is decidedly at odds with the dedication that precedes it. The Irish subject of her book is immediately introduced in the opening sentence, in which Butler declares that among her characters are '*two of the most Potent Monarchs of the* Milesian *Race, in that Ancient Kingdom of* Ireland' (p. 39). Here, the striking clash of cultures is epitomized by a single word in Butler's allusion to the 'Milesian' race. In his dedication, Gildon had written of those '*Milesian Tales*, which so charm'd Antiquity it self' (p. 37) but Butler's reference was not to the classical world so reassuringly familiar to eighteenth-century English readers. Butler had in mind, rather, the mythical origins of Ireland. Here, the name derives from Milesius (Míl Espáine), a fabulous Spanish king, whose sons supposedly invaded Ireland around 1300 BC. Debate concerning the Milesian ancestry of the Irish, which would rage among antiquarians later in the eighteenth century, was not unknown in 1716 but was largely confined to learned or polemical works, such as Sir James Ware's *De Hibernia et Antiquitatibus eius Disquisitiones* (1654) or Roderick O'Flaherty's *Ogygia; seu, Rerum Hibernicorum Chronologia* (1685). While Gildon, in the epistle dedicatory, had evoked Heliodorus, Aristotle, Virgil, Horace and other Greek and Latin authors, in defence of the value of Butler's book, the author herself is drawing on a source utterly unfamiliar to Gildon and virtually all other Englishmen and women of the day: the *Foras Feasa ar Éirinn* (written *c.*1634), by the Roman Catholic priest, Seathrún Céitinn (*c.*1580–*c.*1644), known in English as Geoffrey (or Jeoffrey) Keating. Remarkably enough, the *Foras Feasa* (*A Basis of Knowledge about Ireland*) had not even found its way into print in 1716, either in Irish or English. It would only appear, in fact, seven years later in a large folio volume, in English translation, published in London.[17]

Irish Tales is arguably unique, therefore, in all English-language fiction in so directly linking modern English-language print culture and the older Irish-

17 *The General History of Ireland … collected by the learned Jeoffry Keating, D.D., faithfully translated from the original Irish Language, with many curious Amendments taken from the Psalter of Tara and Cashel, and other authentick Records, by Dermo'd* [sic] *O Connor, Antiquary of the Kingdom of Ireland* (London, 1723). For the fullest modern account of Keating and his work, see Bernadette Cunningham, *The World of Geoffrey Keating: history, myth and religion in seventeenth-century Ireland* (Dublin: Four Courts Press, 2000); see also Diarmaid Ó Catháin, 'Dermot O'Connor, Translator of Keating', *Eighteenth-Century Ireland*, 2 (1987), 67–87 (69–70) and Clare O'Halloran, *Golden Ages and Barbarous Nations: Antiquarian Debate and Cultural Politics in Ireland,* c.*1750–1800* (Cork: Cork University Press in association with Field Day, 2004), esp. pp 14–21.

language bardic manuscript culture. Keating's *Foras Feasa* was perhaps the last major European historical work to have circulated in manuscript, rather than in printed, form yet it was demonstrably Sarah Butler's most important source for the historical material she deploys in the thoroughly modern form of the novel. Or, to put the point the other way round, the first appearance in print of sections of Keating's major history – based on his extensive reading of Irish-language chronicles, including the *Lebor Gabála* (*Book of Invasions*), whose account of the successive invasions of Ireland provides the framework for Keating's own work – is to be found in a work of English-language prose fiction.[18]

Sarah Butler's insistence that her work seeks to conflate historical writing and fiction is evident from her opening sentence which declares of the 'Transactions' making up the lives of two Irish monarchs that 'although I have cloath'd it with the Dress and Title of a Novel; yet (so far I dare speak in my own behalf, that) I have err'd as little from the Truth of the History, as any perhaps who have undertaken any thing of this Nature' (p. 39). That late-seventeenth and early-eighteenth century fiction characteristically mixed fictional and historical materials is well established. Among earlier examples of Irish fiction, Robert Boyle drew on a story from St Ambrose's *De virginibus* (377), rehearsed in John Foxe's *Acts and Monuments* (*The Book of Martyrs*), for his *The Martyrdom of Theodora, and of Didymus* (1687), while the anonymous author of *Vertue Rewarded; or, The Irish Princess* (1693) made use not only of contemporary accounts of the Williamite wars in Ireland between 1689 and 1691 but also took substantial amounts of material from a recent translation of the Inca Garcilaso de la Vega's *Comentarios reales* (1609, 1617), for an interpolated tale of the Spanish conquest of the Incas, told by a south American Indian woman.[19] In England, Daniel Defoe would quarry official records in order to recreate the events of 1665 in *A Journal of the Plague Year* (1722) and histories including Bulstrode Whitlocke's *Memorials of the English Affairs* (1682) and the earl of Clarendon's *History of the Rebellion* (1702–4) for his *Memoirs of a Cavalier* (1720). What unites these authors, though, is their shared use of printed sources. No other contemporary work of fiction in English, by contrast, drew its materials from manuscript sources.

It is difficult to overestimate how unfamiliar such materials were in early eighteenth-century England or even among English-speaking Irishmen and women. True, translation of Keating's Irish-language text had begun as early as 1635, and other translations too were made, into both English and Latin, circu-

18 The *Lebor Gabála* is a compilation of five works dating from as early as the eighth century and collected in the eleventh century, which had been recently edited by the Franciscan Mícheál Ó Cléirigh (*c.*1590–1643).

19 See George Story, *An Impartial History of the Wars in Ireland* (1691; expanded ed. London, 1693), and Inca Garcilaso de la Vega, *The Royal Commentaries of Peru*, trans. Sir Paul Rycaut (London, 1688). For 'The Story of Faniaca', see *Vertue Rewarded; or, The Irish Princess*, ed. Ian Campbell Ross and Anne Markey (Dublin: Four Courts Press, 2010), pp 72–96.

lating in Ireland, along with manuscript copies in Irish (there were some 30 known copies in existence by 1700).[20] Yet Thomas Harte, who made a transcription of Keating's work, wrote to his son, relating how it had been:

> my chance to light upon Dr Keting's Irish History of the Kings of Ireland, and for as much as I had never seene any thing of that kind before, and that what our English authors had delivered concerning the antiquities of this Kingdome is very lame and defective and for the most part fabulose as built upon a bad foundation layd by Giraldus Cambrensis who made it his business to extenuat the worth of the Irish and advance that of his Kinsmen and countrymen beyond measure.[21]

Outside of Ireland, even the most learned antiquarians were only gradually becoming familiar with Keating's work, the Welsh scholar Edward Lhuyd purchasing a translation near Killarney in 1700.[22] Much of the apologia Butler offers for her work in the preface would, then, have been utterly unfamiliar to the first purchasers of *Irish Tales* in 1716. The author's passionate defence of the civility of pre-Norman Ireland, which lies at the heart of her work, therefore needed to communicate itself clearly and powerfully. Defending the elegance of the language used by her lovers – this in truth is highly artificial and owes a great deal not only to the diction of heroic romance but also to the contemporary stage, since many of the speeches of the novel's two young lovers scan perfectly as blank verse – Butler contrasts the past and present states of her country, vehemently denying that her fellow countrymen and women were always 'so Rude and Illiterate a People', and arguing that 'altho' they may seem so now, in the Circumstances they lie under, (having born the heavy Yoke of Bondage for so many Years, and have been Cow'd down in their Spirits) yet ... once *Ireland* was esteem'd one of the Principal Nations in *Europe* for Piety and Learning' (p. 39).

Although she does not use the full phrase herself, Butler was in fact mounting a defence of Ireland as *Insula sanctorum et doctorum* or The Island of Saints and

20 The first English-language translation of *Foras Feasa* was undertaken by the catholic scholar, Michael Kearney of Ballylusky, in 1635. The Royal Irish Academy holds a 1668 copy, made by Domhnall mac Thomáis Uí Shuilleabháin, of Kearney's translation (RIA MS 24 G 16). Copies of another English-language translation, completed by the 1680s by an unknown scribe, are held in a number of locations including the National Library of Ireland, Trinity College Dublin, Marsh's Library, Armagh Public Library, the Bodleian Library, and the British Library. A portion of a third English-language translation, found in the papers of Luke Wadding (1588–1657), the Franciscan founder of St Isidore's College in Rome, is held in the Mícheál Ó Cléirigh Institute in University College Dublin. See Cunningham, *Geoffrey Keating*, ch. 10, pp 173–200.

21 See N. Ní Shéaghdha, *Catalogue of Irish Manuscripts in the National Library of Ireland, Fasc. VII* (Dublin: Dublin Institute for Advanced Studies, 1982), pp 13–14, quoted by Diarmaid Ó Catháin, 'Dermot O'Connor', 70.

22 Cunningham, *Geoffrey Keating*, pp 190–1.

Scholars. In this apologia for ancient and modern Ireland, Butler is very much in sympathy with Keating whose *Foras Feasa* was written, at least in part, as an attempt to counteract the many hostile English-authored accounts of Ireland that provided the basis of British knowledge about Ireland: works by Edmund Spenser, Edmund Campion, and Meredith Hanmer, among others.[23] Drawing on another historical source by an Irish author, Peter Walsh's *A Prospect of the State of Ireland* (1682), Butler goes further, asserting 'that once *Ireland* was esteem'd one of the Principal Nations in *Europe* for Piety and Learning; having formerly been so Holy, that it was term'd *The Island of Saints*; and for Learning so Eminent, as all their Chronicles make out, and some others who were not of that Nation, as **Bede* and †*Camden* do avouch for them' (p. 40).[24] It is with unmistakeable national pride that Butler proceeds to rehearse the role of Ireland in preserving and developing European intellectual life in the high middle ages and, especially, the part played by monks like St Columbanus in spreading Christianity and learning through the foundation of monasteries of Luxeuil and Bobbio, in modern France and Italy respectively. To clinch her point – and the general hostility of the principal seventeenth-century English accounts of Irish 'barbarity' makes her passion wholly comprehensible – Butler reminds her English readers that their ancestors had learned the form and manner of writing itself from the example of Irish, again giving Camden and even the generally unsympathetic Spenser as her sources.

In *Irish Tales*, however, Butler is concerned to do much more than mount a tardy defence of Ireland's past greatness, combining her account of ancient Irish civility and resistance to northern invasion with a parallel history of her own times. The struggle between William, Prince of Orange, and James II for the Irish and British thrones, fought out in Ireland, had ended with the defeat of the Jacobite forces at the siege of Limerick in 1691. Beginning in the 1690s, penal legislation – the Penal Laws – was introduced with the explicit aim of restraining the political, religious and economic rights of the Roman Catholics of Ireland (similar legislation affected the rights of the minority Roman Catholic community in protestant England). These laws included the exclusion of Roman Catholics from parliament, the armed forces, and the law. Roman Catholics could not educate their children in Ireland, nor send them abroad to be educated, nor take a university degree. A series of laws was passed aimed at disarming Roman Catholics in Ireland, making it impossible – with rare exceptions – for them to own firearms, swords, or a horse worth more than £5. Even

23 See, for instance, *The Historie of Ireland, collected by three learned authors, viz. Meredith Hanmer, Doctor in Divinitie; Edmund Campion sometime Fellow of St. Johns Colledge in Oxford; and Edmund Spenser, Esq*. (Dublin, 1633).

24 Butler here gives her sources as St Bede's *Ecclesiastical History of the English People* (731) and Camden's *Britannia* (1586; 5th ed. 1600), though her precise references make it apparent that she was quoting from Peter Walsh's *A Prospect of the State of Ireland* (London, 1682), p. 56 n. (a).

in Anne's reign, the drafting of the penal laws reveals fears not simply of riots or civil disorder but of full-scale rebellion, so that special measures could be brought into operation 'in case invasion or intestine war is likely'.[25] In 1715, the year of the Jacobite rebellion, further laws were put on to the statute books, concerning the raising of militias, the preamble stating that 'there have been frequent rebellions and insurrections formerly raised in this kingdom by the popish inhabitants, [so that] there is just reasons to apprehend that the main body of papists may hereafter again endeavour to disturb the publick peace and tranquillity'.[26] It is within the context of this legislation that the significance and power of Sarah Butler's narrative of Irish resistance to foreign invasion can most fully be understood.

The Ireland whose rights Butler seeks to defend is also, however, a country characterized by its population's stubborn attachment to Roman Catholicism, despite post-Reformation attempts to convert the country to Anglicanism by evangelism or coercion or both. Among laws aimed directly at the practice of catholicism in Ireland were those banishing the hierarchy, along with members of religious orders (such as monks and friars), under pain of high treason. In an attempt to lessen the number as well as economic power of Roman Catholics, laws were passed 'to prevent Protestants intermarrying with Papists',[27] as well as offering inducements to Roman Catholics who became communicating members of the Church of Ireland.[28] In the reign of Queen Anne, who succeeded William III in 1702, legislation was enacted with the design of reducing still further the amount of land in Roman Catholic hands. So too were laws against popular catholic observances, such as pilgrimages to sites such as St Patrick's Purgatory on Station Island in Lough Derg, Co. Donegal or to holy wells, and devotions that involved crosses, devotional pictures or religious inscriptions. Again, it is against this background that some of the most powerfully articulated sentiments of the novel are best grasped. Unlike modern historians, Butler and her contemporaries understood the Viking destruction of monasteries and churches as the sacreligious acts of a pagan people. This, certainly, is the understanding of her characters. When her father, the king of Meath, proposes she marry the Viking leader Turgesius, Dooneflaith replies scornfully:

> 'What, Wed a Tyrant! one whose wicked Hands have ransack'd all our Holy Temples, demolish'd all our Altars! burnt all our Churches, and raz'd our Monasteries, Ravish'd our Nuns, slain our Pious Priests, and thrown the very Sacred Host it self to the Dogs; whose Tyranny has Murder'd our Nobles, and fir'd our Towns and Cities!' (p. 63).

25 8 Anne c. 3 (1709), sects. 34–6.

26 2 George I c. 9 (1715), sects. 1–3.

27 9 William III c. 3 (1697), sects 4–5; 2 Anne c. 6 (1703), sect. 5; 8 Anne c. 3 (1709), sect. 14, among others.

28 2 Anne c. 6 (1703), sect. 12.

Whatever the motives of the Scandinavian invaders, the passage reflects angrily on the penal legislation that drove catholics from their places of worship, expelled priests and other religious, and included an act for the abjuration of transubstantiation. The history of protestant antagonism to catholicism from the time of the Reformation through the seventeenth century to the present day is similarly evoked in the account of Turgesius's violent reaction to the disappearance of Murchoe, both political enemy and rival for the hand of Dooneflaith. The Danish tyrant, Butler declares, did not 'spare either Monastery or Church that stood in his way, lest he should take Sanctuary in them. He likewise put to Death all their Priests, and plac'd Heathen Lay-Abbots in every Cloister. Nor did his fury spare either Sex or Age, whom he thought favour'd his Concealment' (pp 57–8). Within *Irish Tales* as a whole, such passages are rare but the fact that they are there at all within months of the 1715 Rebellion, for their role in which Jacobite prisoners were executed, imprisoned or transported, is striking.[29]

The standpoint from which *Irish Tales* defended Ireland and the Irish nation was, moreover, a very particular one. Like Keating, the name Butler denoted Old English ancestry: that is, the Butlers were of Norman, not Gaelic, descent but many continued to adhere to the catholic faith. Though her use of a novel makes her decidedly unusual, in promoting a particular view of Irish history the author of *Irish Tales* not only follows Keating, Peter Walsh and Roderick O'Flaherty in the seventeenth century but notably anticipates later Irish catholic historians, including Charles O'Conor and the abbé James MacGeoghegan, who do likewise.[30] In analysing the full range of eighteenth-century Irish historical writing, Jacqueline R. Hill suggested categories such as 'sceptical Protestant', 'beleaguered Protestant', 'enlightened Catholic', and 'long-suffering Catholic'.[31] Accepting these admittedly imprecise categories, we can nevertheless identify Butler as a 'long-suffering Catholic', a category represented in later eighteenth-century historiography by, among others, the abbé James MacGeoghegan whose Jacobite *Histoire de l'Irlande* (Paris, 1758–63), recalled the events of the previous century, notably the Flight of the Wild Geese (that is, the flight into exile of Irish soldiers in the service of the defeated James II, as part of the terms of the Treaty of Limerick) in its dedication 'Aux troupes irlandoises au service de la France'.

29 Of seven peers convicted of high treason and sentenced to death, two were finally executed: the earl of Derwentwater and Viscount Kenmuir; most other prisoners had their death sentences commuted but some scores were less fortunate, while hundreds of rebels were imprisoned or transported.

30 See Keating, *Foras Feasa*, Walsh, *Prospect*, O'Flaherty, *Ogygia*; James MacGeoghegan, *Histoire de l'Irlande ancienne et moderne*, 3 vols (Paris, 1758–63), and Charles O'Conor, *Dissertations on the Antient History of Ireland* (1753; 2nd ed. Dublin, 1766).

31 Jacqueline R. Hill, 'Popery and Protestantism, Civil and Religious Liberty: The Disputed Lessons of Irish History 1690–1812', *Past and Present* 118 (February 1988), 96–129 (105, 106, 109, 111).

Whatever her background or political agenda, however, the author of *Irish Tales* bore in mind that she was writing not an historical tract but a novel. The entire passage concerning ancient Irish civility arises from the author's desire to defend the 'Passionate and Elegant' language used by her young lovers, Murchoe and Dooneflaith. Such language was necessary, Butler believed (doubtless correctly), since it was by expressing themselves in the language of heroic romance that the young prince and his princess would attract the sympathy of novel readers. Much of the narrative of *Irish Tales* is in fact concerned with the love of the daughter of one Irish provincial king for the son of another. That the consummation of their love is ultimately thwarted is just one of the ways in which Butler manifests her originality as a writer of prose fiction.

Amatory fiction – that is, stories dealing with all the variations and frustrations of desire, many of them written by women – dominated the market for fiction in the late-seventeenth and early-eighteenth centuries. Popular works such as Aphra Behn's *Love-Letters between a Noble-Man and His Sister* (1684–7) and Delarivier Manley's *New Atalantis* (1709) provided readers with voyeuristic excitements and the pleasures of the text, but, as scandalous chronicles that represented historical personages and political events, they also oscillated between the public and the private, so encouraging a practice of double reading. Along with other contemporary fiction, Sarah Butler's *Irish Tales* is part of a world in which, as one critic has remarked, 'the separate spheres of a male public world and a private female world have not yet crystallized'.[32]

In *Irish Tales*, Sarah Butler impressively intertwines public and private narratives. Tracing the development of the love between Dooneflaith and Murchoe against the ominous background of constant warfare, *Irish Tales* both invokes literary convention, in the familiar pull between personal desire and public duty, but also interrogates it. Here both heroine and hero repeatedly subordinate desire to duty, initially in obedience to the commands of their respective fathers. In Butler's fiction, however, the emphasis on the division between the private and public spheres transcends gender differences, portraying the personal and political as complementary considerations, rather than as competing feminine and masculine principles. (By contrast, Jane Barker's *Love's Intrigues* opens with

32 Jacqueline Pearson, 'The short fiction (excluding *Oroonoko*)', in Derek Hughes and Janet Todd (eds), *The Cambridge Companion to Aphra Behn* (Cambridge: Cambridge University Press, 2004), p. 196. Both Ros Ballaster in her *Seductive Forms: Women's Amatory Fiction from 1684 to 1740* (Oxford: Clarendon Press, 1992), and John Richetti in *The English Novel in History, 1700–1780* (London: Routledge, 1999) describe a shift, occurring from the early- to the mid-eighteenth century, away from the 'double voiced' fiction of the early period, with its address to 'knowing' readers (terms used by Richetti in relation to Behn [p. 22]), and towards the adoption of the conventions of domestic fiction. For a recent reconsideration of the ideology of separate spheres and the emergence of the early novel, see Betty A. Schellenberg, *The Professionalization of Women Writers in Eighteenth-Century Britain* (Cambridge: Cambridge University Press, 2005).

direct reference to 'King James's Affairs' and war in Europe, and it is as a distraction from the apprehension aroused by war, and the fears of women for their male relatives, that the narrator is encouraged to give an account of the 'Adventures' of her early years.)[33] In *Irish Tales*, the eschewal of conventional gender attributes is seen most strikingly, perhaps, in the tearful complaints of the pining Murchoe who, faced with separation from his beloved, contemplates suicide, while the resolute Dooneflaith, though equally distressed by the separation from her lover, accompanies her father to battle. In spatial terms, too, the novel refuses the separation into public and private spheres as the scene shifts from Maolseachelvin's court, where Dooneflaith retreats to the garden, only to be accosted by an angry Turgesius, and the court of Brian Boru, where prince Murchoe's movements in his own chamber are monitored by 'all who look'd in at the Keyhole of the Door to see what he did' (p. 78). Virtuous desire, in the form of Dooneflaith and Murchoe's mutual love, subordinated to the call of duty, is distinguished in *Irish Tales* from the destructive desire of the lustful Turgesius, which blinds him to the public consequences of his actions, and will lead to his downfall.

The complex relationship between public and private in *Irish Tales* manifests itself particularly in what Clíona Ó Gallchóir – rightly attaching considerable importance to this aspect of the novel – has termed the heroine's 'virtuous eloquence'. Ó Gallchóir's further argument that this eloquence should be interpreted in terms 'other than the allegorical representation of Jacobitism and Hanoverianism' and as an inscription of private virtue and 'distinct subjectivity', tragically rejected by the public world of the novel, does, however, require some modification.[34] Through their eloquence, each of the lovers positions both self and other as a character to be understood in both private and public dimensions. In her vivid assertion that, if forced to marry Turgesius, she will pierce her heart and 'spurt the reaking stream full in his hated Face' (p. 61), Dooneflaith associates herself with the justified violence of Old Testament heroines such as Judith, the beheader of Holofernes, and liberator of her people. In a softer vein, and one that resonates with the book's catholicism, Murchoe makes his lover a type of the Virgin Mary, saying that her tears 'would largely expiate the Sins of all Mankind' (p. 54). In stark contrast to much contemporary fiction, however, *Irish Tales* does not conclude with virtue receiving its anticipated reward. Balancing public responsibility against private loss, the novel suggests that the pursuance of patriotic principles will inevitably demand personal sacrifice. So, while the fiction's political narrative concludes with a powerful vindication of Irish sover-

33 Jane Barker, *Love's Intrigues: or, the History of the Amours of Bosvil and Galesia, as related to Lucasia, in St Germains Garden* (London, 1713), p. 2.

34 Clíona Ó Gallchóir, 'Foreign Tyrants and Domestic Tyrants: the Public, the Private and Eighteenth-Century Irish Women's Writing', in Patricia Coughlan and Tina O'Toole (eds), *Irish Literature: Feminist Perspectives* (Dublin: Carysfort Press, 2008), pp 17–38 (30, 31).

eignty, its personal drama finds the lovers separated forever by the death of Murchoe in battle. In its concluding sentence, 'Thus did that Warlike and Ancient Kingdom free itself from the Tyranny of its mortal Enemy the *Danes*' (p. 93), *Irish Tales* suggests in a manner unusual for its time and genre the insignificance of personal sacrifice in comparison with the demands of the public good.

In its privileging of public over private concerns, *Irish Tales* ends as it begins. The novel's opening sentence, 'Lasting and terrible were the bloody Wars which the Ancient *Irish* sustain'd against the powerful *Danes*' (p. 43), is insistent in its stress on the historical narrative, taking the reader from a moment of subjection in the past to foreign invasion to present victory at Clontarf. Butler's use of Keating's *Foras Feasa*, along with Walsh's *Prospect* and others is, however, more complex than can be understood merely by identifying the direct sources for many passages in the novel.[35] The period covered by *Irish Tales* extends for the best part of two centuries, though the novel's characters barely age at all. The way in which Butler constructs this unlikely narrative is in fact as bold as it is ingenious. The princess Dooneflaith is the daughter of the king of Meath, Maolseachelvin; her lover is son of a king of Leinster, Brian Boru. In the novel, as in history, Dooneflaith is sought as bride – or in the absence of her father's consent as concubine – by the Danish warrior and ruler, Turgesius. It is her father who conceives of a plot to outwit the Danish tyrant by sending in the place of his daughter and her retinue armed young men, in women's dress (though based on historical sources, the episode notably complements the novel's questioning of conventional gender attributes). The story of the desire of Turgesius (Turges, in the more familiar modern usage) – first told by the chronicler, Gerald of Wales (*c.*1146–1220x23), author of *Topographia Hibernica* (*The Topography of Ireland*) – is related by Keating, though with a conclusion that differs from that of Gerald's, and is traceable to other sources.[36] In terms of seventeenth- and eighteenth-century historical accounts, this part of the narrative could easily be called 'historical', since little of the retelling is significantly different from the various and varied versions of the episode in other sources.

Where Butler departs radically from her sources is in inventing the love affair between Dooneflaith and Murchoe, the son of Brian Boru. Brian Boru (*c.*941–1014) lived a full century after Maolseachelvin, father of Butler's Dooneflaith. The Maolseachelvin who was father of Dooneflaith is known to modern historians as Máel Sechnaill I (d. 862); the Maolseachelvin who, in *Irish Tales*, both precedes and follows Brian Boru as high-king of Ireland is, rather, Máel Sechnaill II (d. 1022). Butler's conflation of these two kings into a single figure in her fiction results, however, not from indifference to history but from

35 For Butler's use of Keating and Walsh as sources, see 'Notes', passim.

36 Keating drew both on Gerald's account and also on the early-twelfth century *Cogadh Gaedel re Gaillaibh*; see note to p. 41, 'Turgesius', below.

a desire to construct a historical narrative that emphasizes Irish national resistance to foreign invasion. The author's admission that her account is compressed is, it must be acknowledged, more than a little disingenuous:

> I have, I must confess, omitted several Remarkable Passages, and Twenty four of the Twenty five Battles which *Bryan Boraimh* Fought in his Reign and won; but yet I have not foisted in any thing, that might be injurious to the Truth, in their Places, and have only made a Compendium of Things as tho' done in four or five Years time, which perhaps were Transacting half so many score. (p. 41)

Far from being random, in fact, Butler's collapsing of two distinct periods of Irish history – moving from the Danish invasions under Turgesius to the final defeat of the Danes at the battle of Clontarf – is managed with considerable elegance, in the interests of the author's political agenda. It is one of the features of Keating's *Foras Feasa* that the author eschewed the annalistic approach to the Irish past characteristic of Mícheál Ó Cleirígh's almost exactly contemporary *Annála Ríoghachta Éireann* in favour of a continuous narrative that took its shape from the *Lebor Gabála* or *Book of Invasions*. The historian Peter Walsh, who provided a subsidiary source for Butler, followed Keating in his *Prospect* and, almost certainly, suggested the collapsed narrative time-scale that is so effective in fictional terms in *Irish Tales*, since he takes the reigns of the two Máel Sechnaills as the limits of a period in which God permitted 'those Ministers of his Vengeance, the *Norvegians*, *Danes*, and their other barbarous Heathen Associats known to us only by the name of *Oostmans*, or *Easterlings* … to continue their Inundations in *Ireland*, to Plague a Rebellious ungrateful Generation of Christians, and plague 'em now for a hundred and fifty years more compleat'.[37] What is important for Butler, in choosing to omit a century of Irish history, as in omitting twenty-four of the twenty-five battles fought by Brian Boru, is the need to produce a clear narrative of Irish resistance to foreign invasion. In fact, as her sources told her, the hundred years she passes over were marked primarily by struggles for supremacy among provincial kings, rather than battles of national resistance against the Danes. In order to obscure the internecine warfare that characterized tenth-century Ireland Butler concentrates on a single, celebrated battle, the battle of Clontarf, which marked the end of Danish or Viking pretensions to hold political power in Ireland and which confirmed the high-kingship of Ireland.[38] To read the account of the period from the late-ninth to early-eleventh century

37 Walsh, *Prospect*, pp 152–3. Walsh is correct in noting that the period extended to around 150 years rather than the 40 or 50 to which Butler admits.

38 Máel Sechnaill II had been high-king (*ard-rí*) of Ireland until he was deposed by Brian Boru in 1002 but resumed the kingship after Brian was killed at Clontarf, reigning until his death in 1022.

in Keating is to become aware of complex, shifting loyalties and fierce antagonisms between the Irish provincial kings; to read Butler is to recognize the legacy of such antagonisms but also to encounter the author's insistence on the need to subordinate provincial or personal interests to the well-being of Ireland as a whole.[39]

Read in such a manner, *Irish Tales* quickly reveals its contemporary political relevance. In the early-eighteenth century, the history of Ireland from the time of the Norman conquests was often understood in terms of fiercely national resistance to invasion, whether by Henry II, Elizabeth, Cromwell or William III, over the course of many centuries.[40] The decisive battles of the struggle between James II and William III for the thrones of England, Scotland, and Ireland were fought in Ireland: at Aughrim, the Boyne, and at the siege of Limerick. In 1715, Jacobite loyalists hoped for a return of the Stuarts, in the person of Prince James Francis Edward Stuart, son of James II, and known to his supporters as King James III. The first Jacobite rebellion failed – as would the '45 led by Prince Charles Edward Stuart, 'Bonnie Prince Charlie' – but Butler's construction of an Ireland subjected to waves of invaders whom it would, one day, expel for good had its roots deep in the desires of the Gaelic, catholic majority within the country, now suffering under the penal legislation that had severely limited the political, religious and economic freedoms of Roman Catholics since their gradual introduction in the two decades since 1697.

Even if one holds that early-eighteenth-century fiction prepared readers to negotiate between public and private spheres, and to recognize doubled forms of address, it is still difficult to assess how much of Butler's parallel history the first readers of *Irish Tales* would have understood. In a consideration of Jane Barker's Jacobite fiction that includes discussion of *Irish Tales* as a kindred text, Kathryn R. King has written elegantly of how these works might appeal to those attuned to the requisite 'interpretative codes' and thereby nourish 'various estranged communities – Tory, Catholic and Jacobite'.[41] Against this, however, there is the conflicting evidence that even Charles Gildon, who arranged for publication of *Irish Tales*, barely perceived the work's political allegory. How else

39 The dangers of internal rivalry within Ireland are not entirely glossed over by Butler who is faithful to her sources in relating the role played at the battle of Clontarf by Maolmordh MacMurchoe, the king of Leinster, who sides with the Danes, suffering both defeat and death as a consequence (pp 90–1).

40 In the later-eighteenth century, this emphasis on invasion was played down by protestant historians who, in their desire to stress the legitimacy of their own position in the country, preferred to speak of the 'arrival' of Henry II in Ireland; see, for instance, Jacqueline Hill, 'Politics and the Writing of History: the Impact of the 1690s and 1790s on Irish Historiography', in D. George Boyce, Robert Eccleshall, and Vincent Geoghegan (eds), *Political Discourse in Seventeenth- and Eighteenth-Century Ireland* (Houndmills: Palgrave, 2001), pp 227–31.

41 King, *Jane Barker*, pp 148, 179. More tendentiously, King also argues that the fact that Edmund Curll marketed Jacobite fiction is 'evidence of a robust demand' (p. 177).

can we account for the dedication of the book to the paymaster general of the Hanoverian forces in the 1715 Rebellion? Yet if the contemporary success of *Irish Tales* – new editions of the work would appear in London and Dublin in 1719, 1727 and 1735 – did not depend solely on its Irish national concerns, then it exercised a curious appeal to contemporary readers of prose romance. Sarah Butler recognized so much herself when she wrote:

> I have constrain'd my self, contrary to the Custom of most who write these sorts of Essays [i.e. novels], to make my Lovers die unmarried; since I could find no Authority to the contrary. And I should indeed have been very willing to have embrac'd the Opportunity (could I have found any colour for it) of making them, after so many Misfortunes, to have ended their Trouble in the Married Bed. (p. 41)[42]

So, while Butler's account of the love of Dooneflaith and Murchoe brings her work closer to the interests of novel readers in the early decades of the eighteenth century it simultaneously denies those readers the happy ending usually reserved for virtuous love, while casting an oblique light on the political narrative. In the course of the novel, Turgesius receives the appellation of 'tyrant' on over a dozen occasions. Ultimately, however, the lovers are denied the marriage both seek not by the barbarous Dane but by the capricious and often arbitrary behaviour of their respective fathers. It is Maolseachelvin and Brian Boru who force their children, repeatedly, to defer their marriage, as political and personal circumstances change, only for all possibility of that marriage to disappear with the death of Murchoe at the battle of Clontarf. Sarah Butler's management of the twin private and public dimensions of her tale is in many ways exemplary for the reader who, interested in the fate of the lovers, is never allowed to forget either the sacrifice the national interest demands, nor the fact that ridding Ireland of the tyrant Turgesius leaves the royal lovers equally subject to the whims of royal power exercised in an arbitrary manner. If *Irish Tales* offered its readers an ideal(ized) Irish Jacobite narrative of virtue rewarded, it also proffered materials for a considerably bleaker contemporary

42 It is perhaps necessary, however, to observe that Sarah Butler is being somewhat disingenuous here, for though none of her readers is likely to have been aware of the fact, Butler's story of the love between Dooneflaith and Murchoe is wholly invented. Quite apart from the fact that, historically, the daughter of Máel Sechnaill I and the son of Brian Boru lived in different centuries, the (unnamed) princess is a shadowy figure in Keating's narrative – the occasion for the tricking and killing of Turgesius and little more – while the son of Brian Boru figures in *Foras Feasa* as warrior but not as lover. The story of Turgesius and the daughter of the king of Meath repeatedly attracted the attention of historians but seemingly the only writer to give the latter a name is the abbé James MacGeoghegan, who calls her 'Melcha': '[Turgesius] aperçut sa fille, nommée Melcha, qui étoit jeune & de figure à plaire', *Histoire de l'Irlande: Ancienne et moderne*, 3 vols (Paris, 1758–63), I, p. 384.

reading in which both Dooneflaith and Murchoe are little more than pawns in a political game played out by their fathers.

The focus on individual feeling and its claims on the reader are what most obviously distinguish Butler's fiction from her source material. In the extended, elaborate, poetic speeches made by both Dooneflaith and Murchoe, protesting their love or bewailing the circumstances that keep them apart, the contemporary reader would certainly have understood the work as an heroic romance where, in the words of William Congreve's preface to *Incognita*: 'Constant Loves and invincible Courages of Hero's, Heroins, Kings and Queens, Mortals of the first Rank, and so forth; where lofty Language, miraculous Contingencies and impossible Performances, elevate and surprize the Reader into a giddy Delight'.[43] Few contemporary readers, however, were likely to have found 'giddy Delight' in the frustrated marriage of Dooneflaith and Murchoe, or in the deaths of the lovers, Murchoe slain in battle and Dooneflaith dying on hearing the news. That Murchoe and Dooneflaith die without achieving the happy ending their story implies perhaps offers a check on an overly optimistic reading of contemporary events on the part of Sarah Butler. If the Battle of Clontarf put an end to Danish rule in Ireland, then national aspirations to self-determination had suffered repeated setbacks as waves of Anglo-Norman, Elizabethan, Cromwellian, and Williamite settlers had taken their place.[44] In 1716, Irish Jacobites were once more waiting for the return of the king across the water.

How, then, might *Irish Tales* be read today? Here, the distinction made by Michael McKeon between 'progressive' and 'conservative' narratives offers a useful model for, as McKeon argued, 'the transformation of linear into circular movement is a feature of conservative much more than of progressive plotting'.[45] In other words, whereas English historiography of the seventeenth and early-eighteenth centuries characteristically proffered linear accounts of Ireland's progression from native barbarism to English civilization, *Irish Tales* both echoed recent catholic historiography, as it anticipated later-eighteenth century writing by catholics and liberal protestant historians alike, in insisting on a circular movement from Gaelic civilization to its suppression under foreign (that is, Danish and/or English) domination, and to the restoration of learning and true religion as native liberties are, at last, restored: 'Thus did that Warlike and Ancient Kingdom free it self from the Tyranny of its mortal Enemy the *Danes*' (p. 93).

Although *Irish Tales* enjoyed some success over the following two decades, with three further editions, it was perhaps too complex a work of fiction, published

43 William Congreve, 'The Preface to the Reader', *Incognita* (London, 1692), p. viii.

44 For a brief discussion of the association made between *nasión* and *Éireannach*, in the seventeenth century, see Mícheál Mac Craith, 'Literature in Irish, *c.*1550–1690', in Margaret Kelleher and Philip O'Leary (eds), *Cambridge History of Irish Literature*, 2 vols (Cambridge: Cambridge University Press, 2006), I, pp 191–231 (208–10).

45 See Michael McKeon, *The Origins of the English Novel, 1600–1740* (Baltimore and London: Johns Hopkins University Press, 1987), pp 226–36 (p. 230).

at too unlikely a moment, for its full import to be understood in its own day.[46] Paradoxically, Butler's is also a book whose ready accessibility to modern readers is frequently at odds with the complex conventions, historiographical traditions, and allusiveness that governed its writing. Certainly, it is striking that Butler's version of Irish history, her emphasis on Ireland as 'insula sanctorum et doctorum', predated all of those works that modern historians have indicated as important in what one has called 'the wave of enthusiasm for ancient Gaelic civilization which swept over England and Ireland in the first half of the eighteenth century' attributable to 'a new development: the presentation of the Gaelic past, in a positive light, to an English-speaking readership'.[47] So, Sarah Butler anticipated works by Roman Catholic historians such as Hugh MacCurtin in his *A Brief Discourse in Vindication of the Antiquity of Ireland* (1717), as well as Dermot O'Connor's translation of Keating's *Foras Feasa ar Éirinn* as *A General History of Ireland* (1723). Butler likewise anticipated emerging protestant endorsements of positive images of ancient Ireland such as *The Irish Historical Library* (1724) by the Church of Ireland bishop of Derry, William Nicolson, and Bishop Francis Hutchinson's *A Defence of the Antient Historians with a Particular Application of it to the History of Ireland and Great Britain* (1734). What makes *Irish Tales* still more noteworthy, of course, is that Sarah Butler combined her positive revaluation of Irish Gaelic culture with Roman Catholic and Jacobite polemics in a London-published novel.

Blending heroic romance with material dependent on Keating's still unpublished *Foras Feasa ar Éirinn*, Butler telescoped over a century of Irish history in ways that allowed her to be true to her sources – in that she invented little more than the love affair between the fiction's hero and heroine – while producing a simple yet strong narrative of repeated resistance by the natives to foreign attempts to conquer Ireland and of their ultimately successful reassertion of their native liberties and religion. Read in this way, *Irish Tales* embodies, in a work of popular prose fiction, a coherent view of the Irish past based on an important seventeenth-century historiographical account that existed only in manuscripts known to none but a handful of scholars working in Irish or English. It likewise succeeds in articulating a political view of contemporary Ireland at a time when Irish catholics were largely demoralized and Jacobitism a defeated force. For this, and for the unexpectedly complex representation of private desire and public duty in the story of its two royal lovers, *Irish Tales* invites more widespread critical attention from all those interested in the early novel or in eighteenth-century Irish history.

46 The dates of the subsequent editions are, however, suggestive, since 1719 saw the impassioned debate surrounding the Declaratory Act, which sought to restate the supremacy of the parliament in London over the parliament in Dublin, while 1727 marked the death of George I and the accession of his son, George II. The fact that the 1719 and 1727 editions appeared under the title *Milesian Tales* also suggests the possibility that, following the novel's first appearance, readers better understood Butler's reference to the Milesians than Gildon appears to have done.

47 Hill, 'Popery and Protestantism', 102.

A note on the text

The text of the present edition follows, as closely as possible, that of the first edition of *Irish Tales*, using the Trinity College Dublin Library copy OLS 198.0.64 no.13. Emendations to copy-text are listed on p. 110, with the exception that modern practice has been used to indicate direct speech, replacing the eighteenth-century convention of quotation marks running down the left-hand margin of the page.

The first edition of *Irish Tales* was published in London by Edmund Curll and J[ohn] Hooke in 1716. A second edition, identically paginated, but retitled *Milesian Tales* and bearing the imprint 'E. Curll in Fleetstreet and J. Roberts in Warwick-Lane' appeared in 1719. A third edition, also entitled *Milesian Tales*, and with the same pagination, was published in London in 1727, under the imprint of H. Curll; Henry Curll was Edmund Curll's son and his name appeared on imprints during the time his father was imprisoned between November 1726 and February 1728. The fourth edition of the book reverted to the title *Irish Tales* and bore the title-page imprint 'London: Printed, and Dublin Re-printed, and Sold by Ebenezer Rider in George's Lane, 1735'. Although differently paginated, this fourth edition, like the second and third editions, contains no substantive variants.

Irish TALES:

OR,

Instructive HISTORIES for the happy Conduct of LIFE.

Containing the following Events.

VIZ.

I. The Captivated MONARCH.
II. The Banish'd PRINCE
III. The Power of BEAUTY.
IV. The Distrest LOVERS.
V. The Perfidious GALLANT.
VI. The Constant FAIR-ONE.
VII. The Generous RIVAL.
VIII. The Inhuman FATHER.
IX. The Depos'd USURPER.
X. The Punishment of UNGENEROUS LOVE.

By Mrs. SARAH BUTLER.

LONDON: Printed for E. Curll at the *Dial* and *Bible*, and *J. Hooke*, at the *Flower-de-Luce*, both against St. *Dunstan*'s Church in *Fleetstreet*, 1716.

Price 1*s*. 6*d*. Stitch'd, 2*s*. Bound.

THE

Epistle DEDICATORY,*

TO THE

RIGHT HONOURABLE

The Earl of *Lincoln.**

My LORD,

THE Fair Authress* of the following Sheets being Dead, and the Publication of them falling into my Hands, I could not think of any PATRON, under whose Protection, they might with that Advantage I desir'd, venture into the Publick, so properly as your Lordship's. For, where better could HEROIC LOVE, and all the PATRIOT VIRTUES* find a surer and more auspicious Refuge, than under that *Nobleman*'s Protection, whose distinguish'd Honour, and good Sense has render'd him so eminently capable of the *former*; and whose *stedfast Zeal* for his Country's Service in the most dubious, and difficult of Times* has been so conspicuous to all that know any thing of our publick Affairs, as that of your Lordship. Yes, my Lord, that Heroic Firmness and Resolution you discover'd then in your Conduct, has made you the peculiar Darling of all true BRITONS,* of all Lovers of the best of Kings,* and Constitutions. *Resolution*, and *Uncorruptible Faith* are not the common Growth of this Age, which makes every Consideration yield to the poor and mean Prospects of immediate and Personal Advantages, either in Wealth, or in Power and Dignities; and few, very few have been found, whom neither the Malice and ungenerous Persecution of Potent and disappointed Enemies could break, nor all the gilded Baits of Power, Riches, Flattery,

Pleasure, and the other cunning Arts of insinuating into the Minds of the young and uncautious (in which vile Arts, those were no small Proficients, who had then the Publick Management of Affairs)* could corrupt, or give the least shock to; on whose Wiles, tho' many were deceived by them, your Lordship, supported by a perfect Integrity, and just Understanding, look'd down and despis'd.

IT is such a Publick Spirit, such an Understanding, that qualifies a Nobleman to be worthy of the Addresses of the MUSES. For whoever loves his Country, must be pleas'd to see ARTS Flourish, which add to its Glory and its Felicity; since that Country can only be estem'd truly Happy and Great, where ARTS as well as Arms* find publick Encouragement. And of all ARTS, POETRY is perhaps the chief, which deserves the peculiar Care of the *Great* and the *Polite*.

IF we may decide this by what we find in History, it is plain, that where-ever Heroic Fortitude, and Martial Glory have found a distinguishing Success, there POETRY has met with the greatest Indulgence.

ATHENS, which polish'd Mankind by her POETS, was able by her single Valour, under the Conduct of MILTIADES,* with Ten Thousand Men, to defeat some Hundreds of Thousands of *Persians*. ROME in her greatest Glory, and most establish'd Fortune, became a Rival of GREECE in that *Noble Art*, while VIRGIL, HORACE, VARIUS, TUCCA* and many more, found themselves the peculiar Favourites of the ablest Statesman, and most illustrious Emperor* that Nation ever knew.

IT would be no difficult Matter, my Lord, to carry on the Proof of this in a less eminent degree through the several Kingdoms that arose out of the Ruins of the *Roman Empire*, even from *Italy*, to *Hungary*; but that would be a Work of too large an Extent for the narrow Compass of an Epistle. By hinting this here, I only aim at stirring up, if possible, a generous Ambition in our Great Men, of distinguishing themselves in a manner so worthy of Power and Dignity.

I have known a Nobleman, who (I know not by what means) got a popularity for his Generosity, who yet could only justly pretend to an injudicious Profusion; for he has given a Piper Three Hundred Guineas,* when a MAN of LEARNING found but a very mean Gratuity for a most valuable Performance. But several have, indeed, been bountiful to Fidlers, and the *thrilling Throng*, while we have found very few SIDNEYS and SACKVILES,* since we have pretended to Politeness; and yet the many Excellent Products of Poetry, with little or no Encouragement, are a Proof that it is the natural Growth of the Clime,* and with a tolerable Cultivation, might arrive at the greatest Perfection.

THE following Sheets, my Lord, are of this Kind; that is, they are allow'd by the Learned to be a useful sort of POETRY, tho' without the advantageous Harmony of Verse. For as all POETRY is an IMITATION,* as ARISTOTLE justly observes, it is plain that all *Fables* are IMITATIONS of *Actions*, which is the essence of both the DRAMATIC and EPIC POESIE.

BUT this *Prosaic Poetry* is of as ancient a Date as the *Milesian Tales*,* which so charm'd Antiquity it self. The Moderns since the Time of HELIODORUS,* have often vary'd their Form; some Years ago they swell'd them into large Volumes, but of late the general Tast* runs for such as are compriz'd in a much narrower Compass; from whence we derive so many Books of TALES,* which have not yet fail'd of Success. These that follow, in my Opinion, fall not in the least short of the most excellent that have yet appear'd; there being a Pathetic Tenderness, that runs quite through them, supported by a Noble and Heroic Fortitude.

THE Preface will shew your Lordship that their

Foundation is laid on true History,* and the Lady has so artfully Grafted the Fiction upon it, that the whole bears the pleasing Appearance of Truth and Reality.

If they contribute to the Diversion of any Hour of your Lordship's more elegant Leisure, I have my Aim. My Ambition to give this publick Testimony of my Esteem and Value for your Lordship's singular Virtues, would not suffer me to lose the first Opportunity of doing it, unable to delay my Zeal 'till I had something more solid to offer; though perhaps, in Justice, it is not the most unmeritorious Endeavour to contribute to our Diversion; and I hope it will be thus favourably receiv'd by your Lordship from,

My LORD,

Your Lordship's most Humble

and most Obedient Servant,

CHARLES GILDON.

THE

PREFACE.

I HERE present the Reader with some few of those many Transactions which made up the Lives of two of the most Potent Monarchs of the Milesian *Race,* in that Ancient Kingdom of* Ireland: *And although I have cloath'd it with the Dress and Title of a Novel;* yet (so far I dare speak in my own behalf, that) I have err'd as little from the Truth of the History, as any perhaps who have undertaken any thing of this Nature.*

What I have added , is only the Love and Amorous Discourses of Murchoe *and* Dooneflaith;* *whose Name I have presum'd upon, since in the Chronicles and Writings of all those, which I have read, who have Treated on that Subject, make no mention of the Name of* Maolseachelvin's *Daughter;* tho' none af them hardly but take notice of the Story. And finding in Dr.* Ketrius's* Manuscript *that of* Dooneflaith *to be in use at that time, and (if I mistake not) to be the Name of her Mother, I therefore was the more willing to imagin I should not err so much from Truth, as if I had given her a feign'd one, to give that to her Daughter.*

Some (upon what Grounds I know not) would needs have their manner and way of making Love, which I have brought as near as I could to our modern Phrase, to be too Passionate and Elegant for the Irish, *and contrary to the Humours, they alledge, of so Rude and Illiterate a People; when all the while they do not consider, that altho' they may seem so now, in the Circumstances they lie under, (having born the heavy Yoke of Bondage for so many Years, and have been Cow'd down in their Spirits) yet that once* Ireland *was esteem'd one of the Principal Nations in* Europe *for Piety and Learning; having formerly been so Holy, that it was term'd* The Island of Saints;* *and for Learning so Eminent, as all their Chronicles make out, and some others who* *were not of that Nation, as* *Bede, *and* †Camden* *do avouch for them.*

It was so Famous for Breeding, that many from the adjacent Islands, and most parts of the Continent of Europe *came thither for it.*

Insomuch as P. Walsh *says in his Prospect of* Ireland,* *that when any were wanting from their own Country, it came to be a Proverb*, He is gone to *Ireland* to be bred.

And another in the Life of Sulgenus, *has this Distich.*

> Exemplo patrum commotus amori legendi,
> Ivit ad Hibernos Sophia mirabile claros.*

And we find in their Chronicles, that there were Four Great Universities in Ireland,* *viz.* Ardmagh, Cashell, Dunda-Leathghlass, *and* Lismore, *besides many other Colleges of less Note elsewhere; and as* Keting* *in his* Manuscript *has it, in the Reign of* Couchuvair Mac-Donochoe,* *that there were no less than* 7000 *Scholars at one time in one of those Universities*, viz. Ardmagh; *and that they were the* Irish *in those Days who gave a beginning Abroad, as some Writers say, to the Schools of* Oxford. *But it is most certain they did to those of* Paris *and* Pavia,* *and many other great Colleges of Learning in Foregn Parts.*

And both Camden *and* Edmund Spenser *in his* View of Ireland, *page 29.* do acknowledge*, That our Ancestors in *Great Britain* learned the very form and manner of framing their Character for Writing, from *Ireland*.

From what has been said, (tho' not a Tenth part of what might be on this very account) I hop'd I might have liberty to dress their words in as becoming a Phrase as my weak Capacity could frame, or the time that I did it in would allow.

As for the other part of the Story, it is all Historical, and treads only the Path of the true Chronicle, if we may give Credit to my

**Bede* in his *Hist. Anglic.* lib. 3. cap 4, 5, 19 & lib. 4. cap 25. † *Camden Brittan.* p. 730. Edit. Lond. *in fol.* anno. 1607.

Authors, who are Bede, Camden, Heylin, Spenser, Hanmor, Campion, *Dr.* Keting, *Sir* James Ware, Flahertus, *and* P. Walsh.* *I have, I must confess, omitted several Remarkable Passages, and Twenty four of the Twenty five Battles which* Bryan Boraimh *Fought in his Reign and won;* but yet I have not foisted in any thing, that might be injurious to the Truth, in their Places, and have only made a Compendium of Things as tho' done in four or five Years time, which perhaps were Transacting half so many score.**

I have constrain'd my self, contrary to the Custom of most who write these sort of Essays, to make my Lovers die unmarried; since I could find no Authority to the contrary. And I should indeed have been very willing to have embrac'd the Opportunity (could I have found any colour for it) of making them, after so many Misfortunes, to have ended their Trouble in the Married Bed.*

Lastly, since my Design in the beginning was to shew the strange means by which Ireland *was once deliver'd from the Tyranny of* Turgesius* *and the* Danes, *by the Beauty of a Virgin;* I thought it might not be impertinent to the Story, to make the same Maid, tho' in a more vertuous way, be the Instrument of saving it a second time, by infusing of Courage into her Lover, who, we'll suppose for her sake, did things that Day, which almost surpass all belief; tho' at the same time she had little or no part it may be in the Victory. This License I presum'd might lawfully be granted in a Novel.*

Irish TALES.

LASTING and Terrible were the bloody Wars which the Ancient *Irish* sustain'd against the powerful *Danes*;* who, by their vast Numbers, and continual supplies of fresh Men, who Recruited them daily, and were weekly landing at one Port or other, came to their aid, they being then Masters of the Sea, so harass'd and tir'd the long defending Islanders, that at last they were forc'd to submit, and their Provincial Kings become for some small space of Time, Tributaries to the *Dane*.

Turgesius,* the *Danish* Captain General, being a Soldier of invincible Courage, and no less Ambitious, made himself be stil'd Monarch of *Ireland*, and with a Splendid and Magnificent Train of hardy and resolute Warriors, whom Peace and Idleness, the Seeds of Wickedness, and the Mildew of Vertue had rusted into Courtiers, kept his Court in the center of the Country, at *Lough-Ribh*,* near that place, where now stands the Town of *Athlone*.*

He was a Man so skill'd and train'd up in Arms, and Martial Fatigues, that had he only follow'd the Business he profess'd, his Conquests and Victories might have been an everlasting Theme for Ages to come; and had not his Lust like a Canker eaten away the Inscriptions his Sword had engraven, his Victorious Memory might to this day have been the enduring Song of Fame.

Turgesius having subdu'd the best part of the People of this Nation, nay, indeed, we may say all, but a few who knew not how to bow their Necks in subjection to any but a lawful Prince, or stoop to any thing beneath their free Liberties, and Obedience to their own Kings, had betaken themselves to Boggs, Woods, Mountains, Rocks, and inaccessible Places; whose Wisdom and Conduct being back'd with an inimitable Valour, in a few Weeks wrought out their own Infranchizements, and broke the servile Bonds, in which their fellow *Irish* were enslav'd, notwithstanding the mighty Care and Circumspection *Turgesius* us'd to the contrary; for there was not a Hole, or a Corner, much less a Town or a City in the whole Realm, that was capable of it, in which he had not planted a Garrison,* made as he thought, secure by impregnable Fortifications.

All things being order'd in this manner, he began to partake of the Pleasures of Peace, which his long Toil and indefatigable Labours had newly establish'd. Those cruel Wars which had open'd the veins of this distemper'd sick Kingdom, had not yet drain'd one drop of his ill Blood, which corrupting for want of usual Exercise, made him degenerate from the noble Science of War, to practise that of Love; and giving way to his unruly Passion, became in a short time wholly Conquer'd by the fair Eyes of *Dooneflaith*, the Daughter of *Maolseachelvin* King of *Meath*.*

This Lady was one, on whom Nature had lavishly bestow'd all the Graces and Ornaments which could be, to make Humanity adorable; she was so nobly endow'd, and so incomparably Beautiful, that to see her, and not admire her, was impossible; yet was she capable of all the soft sentiments Love could imprint; and had already devoted her Heart to a Man, to whom without blame she might warrantably do, being Prince *Murchoe*,* Eldest Son to *Bryan Boriamh*,* who was afterwards Elected King of all *Ireland*.*

This Prince matchless in his gallant Exploits, was not less to be paralell'd in his Love; it is enough to tell you, he saw the beautiful *Dooneflaith*, and consequently lost his Heart in the sight; but so much awe did her Vertue create in him, that for some time he languish'd in the Torments of his Flame, without daring to utter one word of his Love; and all the while the charming *Dooneflaith* was subject to the same Malady.

Thus for a Time did these two secret Lovers live in Hopes that Fortune would at some time or other, be propitious to their Amours; and altho' they were so enamour'd of each other, yet dar'd not either of them shew the least sign of their Passion. For now *Turgesius* made it his business to win the Heart of this Lady, and *Maolseachelvin* himself was not the last who discern'd it; nor could he any way forbid his Address, knowing how dangerous a thing it might prove, to stand in competition with so mighty and powerful a King. *Murchoe* was not insensible of it, and to his inexpressible Grief, was forc'd in silence to bewail his Misfortunes, and see all the Joy of his Soul Caress'd and Ador'd by another: What Lamentations and Moans would he make when alone? And what Grief would possess him, when he fear'd that his charming *Dooneflaith* might in time consent to the Love of the Tyrant. He became so Melancholy and Troubled, that the whole Court cou'd not but take notice of it; and notwithstanding he us'd all endeavours to stifle his Flame, yet he could not so closely conceal it, but *Turgesius* (for no Eyes are sharper than those of the Jealous) perceiv'd it; and under pretence that he suspected him to be Ill inclin'd to his Government, Banish'd him the Province, which was a far greater Punishment to the young Prince, than had he instantly doom'd him to Die.

Dooneflaith was soon made acquainted with the Misfortune of *Murchoe*, in which she took such part, that she had much ado to refrain falling in a swoon before the King, and was forc'd to feign an Excuse to get from his sight; she went slenderly accompanied, having but two Maids who kept at a distance, into a Garden, at the farther end of which was a Grove, whose melancholy shades seem'd fittest for her Condition; and in which obscurity she might have free Liberty (thinking no body by) to vent her Complaints, while her Women, who seeing her sit down on a Bank, retir'd to an Arbour hard by.

It was not without much trouble, and many endeavours that she could find utterance for her words, her sighs and sobs still hindring her Speech; but at length having by large streams of Tears, which ran down her Cheeks, almost drain'd the Channels of her Eyes, she began to give ease to her Heart, which without vent, must have certainly burst.

'Oh! unfortunate and miserable *Dooneflaith* (saith she) whither wilt thou fly for ease, since *Murchoe*, the peace of thy Soul is banish'd thy sight, and whose presence was the only stay of my Life; what avails Life, or Eyes to me, now that dear Object's gone? Surely this Tyrant who usurps our Throne, has found I love the Prince, and his Jealous Fears have drove him from the Court, that he might also usurp a place in my Heart! Oh! *Murchoe*, *Murchoe*, cou'dst thou but know my Soul; Oh! that my sighs could reach thy distant Ears, and make thee sensible of what I suffer for thee'.

While she was thus complaining to her self, e're she was aware *Turgesius* approach'd her, and found her in tears; just at the same time as *Murchoe*, who behind an adjoyning Hedge had over-heard all she had said, was going to throw himself at her feet; but seeing *Turgesius* arrive, he lay still, as much pleas'd with what he had learnt from *Dooneflaith*'s own mouth, as troubled and afflicted at the coming of so Potent a Rival, who hinder'd him from making known to his Mistriss the sense that he had of her Goodness, and the absolute Power she had gain'd over his Heart.

Dooneflaith was greatly surpriz'd to see one so near her, whom she so much fear'd, and had cause to hate; she would have risen and left the Place to the King; but was prevented, by his taking her by the Hand, and throwing himself down by her; she, not yet well awaken'd from the lulling Cogitations of her dear *Murchoe*, her beautiful Face all cover'd with blushes, was forc'd to sit down by *Turgesius*; who casting a look, which signify'd how much he was concern'd for her Trouble, desir'd her to tell him the cause of it; adding, if it lay in his power to give her Redress, she had no more to do but command him.

Dooneflaith, at the present, was at a loss what Answer to make him; 'till after several Demands, she spoke in this manner.

'My Lord (said she) you urge me to do that, which I fear when perform'd, will displease you. 'Tis not but that I know the Honour you are pleas'd to confer on our Family in vouchsafeing to cast your Affections on me, who so little deserve them; nor is it, but that I have confidence enough in your Kingly Word, that makes me thus scrupulous; but so it is, unless with an Oath you confirm that you will grant my Request, I shall still keep the cause of my Grief to my self'.

Turgesius, was strangely perplex'd in his Mind, to see one, whom he thought he might have commanded, make Capitulations* with him, and so much to distrust the Word of a Monarch, that no less than an Oath would serve to confirm her, He told her, 'That had she not gotten an absolute sway over his Heart, he wou'd never have condescended to a thing the most powerful Prince shou'd never have gained from him; in short, he swore to her By Heaven, and all his Pagan Gods,* that whatever she demanded if it lay in his power should be granted, upon Condition that she would allow him to love her, and give him leave to hope, that in time his Passion might be rewarded'.

'My Lord, (reply'd she) you pretend to grant my request, and tell me my Power is absolute, and yet you confine me to that, which perhaps, of all things in the World is opposite to my quiet; as for your loving me, it lies not in my power to hinder; and as for your hopes that your Passion may be rewarded, is a thing I can willingly suffer, so that you will not by your Power and Authority urge me to Marry you against my consent, and withall, that you would recall the unhappy *Murchoe*, whom I know you have banish'd only for my sake'.

Turgesius after a small pause, answer'd her 'Madam said he altho' your Father should command you to marry me, nay, tho' my Life, and my future Eternal Happiness only depended upon it, yet will I allow you your own liberty, nor ever Wed you, unless you freely consent to it. But as for *Murchoe*'s repeal, it wou'd indeed shew in me too much love, but too little discretion; for I know well, Madam, (says he going on) the *Prince*'s Thoughts are too aspiring, and that so long as he lives in the Province, I must expect neither Peace in my Throne, nor my Love, for I have more sufficient Proofs than bare report, that he Rivals me both in your Heart and my Crown: How much cause have I therefore to hate him? especially now, since you are so much interested for him, I shall but take into my Bosom a Snake,* that when warm'd again with my Favour, will sting me to the Heart, and with his Venom rankle all my Peace and Tranquility; however, to shew you that I pretend not to your Love by that power the Heavens have put into my Hands, I freely consent that he stay still at home, nay even here in our Court, and I shall admit him to use all his Art, and make his Addresses to you, so that I likewise may be heard in my turn'.

Turgesius remained some time silent, in expectation of her Answer, but the blessing his Words had pour'd on her Heart, was too mighty for her Tongue, nor knew she how to return him the Thanks which were due for so noble an Offer, without betraying too much of her Love, but at last overcoming the conflict in her Soul, she utter'd these Words.

'Most renowned Conqueror! your Generosity and Goodness have so far wrought on my Heart, that I fear there is nothing in honour you can demand, that I shall have the ability to deny you: And since it hath pleas'd you to leave all to my choice, I make a farther reference of it to Heaven, who I humbly implore to direct all my Actions; and since so freely you have told me your mind, I will be as liberal of mine, and here solemnly protest, that *Murchoe* has never so much as open'd his Mouth, or made known to me by any means whatsoever, the things which you lay to his Charge'.

Turgesius was pleas'd at these Words, and took his leave of her, with a promise immediately to recall *Murchoe*, whom he told her he believ'd was not departed from Court, it being yet within the limits of the time appointed for his Banishment. *Dooneflaith* return'd him such an answer, as the Nobleness of the Deed did require; she told him he had now took the right course to succeed in his Love; but no sooner was he parted from her, but she began to accuse her own Heart for what she had done, and altho' it was only what her love for *Murchoe* had urg'd her to, yet she could not but lightly condemn the way that she had taken to gain his Repeal; she was too sensible there was no room in her Breast for any but *Murchoe*, and that *Turgesius*, with all his endeavours could never supplant the esteem she had for him; and withal, vow'd in her heart, that if once *Murchoe* shou'd mention his Love, to give him such an answer as should not displease him.

Turgesius had no sooner left her, but at a small distance he espies *Dooneflaith*'s two Women, who at present he knew not, and his curiosity pressing him to see who they were that were most melodiously singing to an Harp,* which they had brought with them into the Garden, Musick being the chief thing that did of late allay the melancholly humour of their Lady; he therefore retir'd under the covert of an Hedge that was by and had but just laid himself down to give attention to the Song, but he espied *Murchoe* with his Sword in his hand; *Turgesius* call'd to his Guards, thinking he had some design on his Person; but *Murchoe* dissipated those fears, by throwing Himself, and his Sword at the Conquerors Feet, without so much as speaking one Word.

Turgesius, who was now in a greater surprize, to see his most mortal Enemy (as he thought him) in so suppliant a posture, and not doubting but that *Murchoe* had had some private Conference with his Mistress, was inflam'd with such Jealousy, that with a fierce and angry tone he pronounc'd aloud these Words, which *Dooneflaith* plainly could hear.

'Ha! Villain, (says he to *Murchoe*) what rash and inconsiderate Thing art thou, whom Heaven has so far deserted, that thou sett'st thy Life at no higher a rate, than thus to presume to approach one, whom so justly thou hast made thy Enemy, and thus darest to infringe those fatal Orders I have given; and thus by intrenching on the liberty I have allowed thee, for thy two days stay to make preparation for thy Banishment, and takest the privilege to interrupt the solitude of her, whom my heart adores, and thereby pull down thy sudden Undoing'.

Murchoe heard these Threats with a Soul all inflam'd with Revenge; but fearing the prejudice of his Mistress, who now he began to hope, held not his Life indifferent, stifled at present his resentment, and tho' at any other time he had a mortal detestation of Flattery, yet now he thought it most expedient for the working his interest with the divine *Dooneflaith*, answer'd him thus.

'Most puissant,* yet haughty *Turgesius*, that Title of Villain you gave me, I renounce, and had you been ten times my Conqueror, would retort it back to thy Face; had I not by accident, and not willingly heard how generously you intend to proceed; it is not this miserable Life I fear to lose, nor is it that Heaven has so far deserted me that makes me Bow at your Feet, nor is this posture I am now in, so Suppliant as it is Thankful; I bow thus low to *Turgesius*, not that I fear the worst he can do, but to return him my thanks for the freedom he gives me in once more seeing *Dooneflaith*, and for the liberty he has granted to permit me to make my humble Addresses to her. Now witness for me all ye Pow'rs above, my Life, my Honour, nay, what's more, my very Soul, I set at nought when She e'er stands in Competition. I must confess, and 'tis the first time I ever taught my Tongue to say it, I Love! I Love, the fair, the charming, virtuous, and all divine *Dooneflaith*; but to my everlasting Torment, I love, without expectance of return; no, were my hopes as great and high as Sinners new absolv'd, I should despair, since I have you for my Rival. What Power have I, dejected banish'd I, when such a resistless Conqueror puts in his claim? A Crown, a Crown, *Turgesius*, I fear will dazzle her fair Eyes, so glittering will the mighty Glory shine, that she will look on no less light'.

'Enough, *Murchoe*, says *Turgesius*, and as I conquer'd thee in Arms, I'll Conquer in my Love; henceforward I'll lay by my Crown, that shall be no title to gain her; nay more, thus far I promise thee, that I will ne'er demand her for my Wife, nor seek her for my Bed on such a Price; Love only shall be currant* Coin, and that I'll lavish to acquire my Ends; take then your Sword, take my Forgiveness, thy own Liberty, and if thou canst, take *Dooneflaith*, I'll condescend so low to call thee Rival now; and since unurg'd thou ownest thou lovest her, thou wilt have punishment enough for all thy Crimes, to see her circled by her own consent within these Arms'.

By this time the Guards were come up, and *Turgesius*, in the sight of them, and *Dooneflaith*, who also was come up when he call'd to his Guards, took *Murchoe* from the Ground, and in the presence of them all, pronounced his Pardon, and the freedom he allow'd him to make his Addresses to *Dooneflaith*.

Dooneflaith was so taken with his generous Proceeding, that she cou'd not with-hold from giving him a thousand

Praises, which made him imagine he had no small Interest in her Heart already; and were as so many stabs in the Breast of *Murchoe*, who now began to think that her pleading for his repeal, was only out of fear that in his absence, he might raise new Forces, and so once more bring *Turgesius*'s Life into hazard: After a walk or two in the Garden, *Turgesius* making *Murchoe* take one of *Dooneflaith*'s fair hands, while he held the other, they went in all together; and now the whole Court was talking of nothing, but the aspiring Love of *Murchoe*, and the noble Condescention of *Turgesius*.

Maolseachelvin was at that instant with *Brian Boraimh*, *Murchoe*'s Father, in consultation how they should shake off the tyrannous Yoak* of this Usurper, when this last adventure came to their Ears, *Maolseachelvin* from thence gather'd some hopes of accomplishing his ends; but *Brian* inwardly accused his Son of disloyalty to his Country, who when he had the Tyrant alone, at his Mercy, prefer'd the love of *Maolseachelvin*'s Daughter, before that of his Honour, and his enthrall'd Kingdom, wherefore they both parted at that time, without coming to any result.

The next day *Turgesius* made his addresses to *Dooneflaith*, but found his reception colder than he imagin'd; wherefore sending for her Father, he discover'd his Mind to him, and contrary to his Promise and Oath to *Dooneflaith*, commanded him to use his utmost endeavours to reduce his Daughter to accept his Love.

Murchoe taking the advantage of *Turgesius*'s Permission, went also to *Dooneflaith*, where he freely open'd his Mind, and discover'd to her all that he had heard from her the day before in the Garden, she saw it was now no time any longer to hide her affections, and to the unspeakable joy of *Murchoe*, confess'd that he had won so much on her heart, that would their Parents consent, she was willing to accept him for her *Husband*; this was not so privately done, but a

Spy whom *Turgesius* had secretly plac'd there to that purpose, made him acquainted with all that had pass'd, which rais'd such confusion in his Soul, that he knew not how to be reveng'd on *Murchoe*, nor what punishment to inflict on *Dooneflaith*; but after many tormenting *Cogitations*, was resolv'd, himself, to be a private Spectator; and if that he found what he fear'd, (and was told him) to be true, to end *Murchoe*'s Life with his own hand.

Wherefore in a day or two after, seeing *Dooneflaith* was inexorable to all his Intreaties, he seem'd to give over his Suit, and now *Murchoe* had the greater liberty of prosecuting his Amours. He had endur'd all the reproaches that an incens'd Father cou'd make him, and had in vain solicited for his consent, and altho' he found his Mistress, and also her Father no ways averse, but rather desiring the Match, yet to his affliction and sorrow he could see no probability of his happiness, since his own Father stood so much against it: No Prayers, nor Intreaties cou'd move him, and he had charged him no more to visit *Dooneflaith* upon that account.

Murchoe, who had yet never known what Disobedience to his Father was, and had never broke the least of his Commands, now saw himself in a miserable condition, either he must loose* the love of his Father, or that of his Mistress, both equally destructive to him, he resolves, at last, to follow his Duty, in hopes that in time his Love thereby would prove more happy; he fail'd not however to pay her his visits, tho' with a Countenance less assur'd than before; and she could not but observe the great alteration that was wrought in his Heart; his Words bore not those soft and sweet accents they were wont, nor did he put that joy on his Face as formerly he had: She could not see so mighty a change, but ask'd to be inform'd of the cause, which with disjointed Words, and heavy Sighs he at length told her.

'O Madam! (says he, *with his Eyes flowing over with Tears*) how unhappy is the wretched *Murchoe*, since even the Heavens conspire to his Misery! and, but that I have reason to hope that I am not altogether indifferent to you, I should not thus pine and waste to my Grave, but boldly at once leap o'er the battlements of Life, and seek for a Death the nearest way'.

Dooneflaith hearing him talk of Death, took him by the hand, and (with a thousand soft charms in her Eyes, tho' half drown'd in Tears, said to him) 'O my Lord! can any thing make your Life so burdensome that you would quit it so long as I love you? can you think of wounding a Heart wherein I have an interest? For so nearly ally'd are all your Sufferings to my self, that not one drop falls from your Eyes, but my Heart answers with the like of Blood: Say then, my *Murchoe*, what has befallen? Has *Turgesius* given you cause of Jealousy? or do you think because I allow of his Visits (which Heaven knows is not in my pow'r to prevent, or I would) that I ever can consent to his Love? No, no, *Murchoe*, not all the Diadems in the World, not all the Monarchs on Earth shall put you from my Heart; there you, and none but you shall Reign, but play not the Tyrant there, and by *Turgesius*'s Example take delight to spoil and ransack what I so freely give',—Here her Sighs broke off her Speech, and rais'd our Lover from the Extasies her tender Words had cast him into.

'Dry up (oh! my Souls dear Treasure, says he) these precious Drops, the moyety of which would largely expiate the Sins of all Mankind; I know thou lov'st me, and am prouder in that Title, than were I Monarch of the Universe; but my Dearest, Charming *Dooneflaith*, thy Love alone but makes me miserable, since I must only see there is an Heaven, but never be admitted to it. My – Oh *Dooneflaith*, my Cruel Father has commanded me to Love no more; no more to talk and spend my happy Hours in thy blest Company, no more to sit and gaze on that dear Face, no more to change soft Looks, and Prattle with our Eyes the Secrets of our Hearts; no more now must I wish for Night, that in my Dreams my *Dooneflaith* may delight me, nor waking in the Morning rise to make me blessed in my Visits to you. *Turgesius* is all merciful and good, his Heart more soft and pliant than my Father's, or were it not, with this Sword I'd–'

Here *Turgesius* came from the Place in which he had over-hear'd all, and was so transported with his Rage, that had not *Dooneflaith* interpos'd, *Murchoe* (e'er he could have turned in his own Defence) had been laid as a Sacrifice to his Anger dead at his feet, nor had he the patience (so much was he blinded with Passion) to stay till he had call'd his Guards; but enter'd alone unarmed all but his Sword.

Murchoe was so lost in his Sorrow, that till he heard *Dooneflaith* shriek out, he saw him not enter, and was ready to save *Turgesius* the pains, and have dy'd of himself, when he saw his Mistress hold his Rival in her Arms; then falling on her Knees (still holding by his Robe) and profusely showring down floods of Tears to save her Lovers Life. 'O *Turgesius*, my Lord, my King and Conqueror, spare, O mighty Monarch, spare my *Murchoe*'s Life, and in exchange I'll give you this of mine; kill not a Man, the Gods themselves wou'd mourn to lose, one whom their utmost Skill can never parallell'.

Turgesius by this time repented him of his entring alone, knowing by that rashness, that he hazzarded a Life, his Love, and a Crown, against a Man most stout, and much beneath him; wherefore going to retreat, he was prevented by *Murchoe*, who by this time had got between him and the Door, and stood ready with his Sword in his Hand to hinder his passage. 'Is this, (says he to him) according to your Kingly Word? Do you esteem your Vows and Oaths so little? Then Heaven refuse me, when I beg its Mercy, if I let slip this opportunity. No, Faithless Tyrant, now I meet thee single, come from thy Buckler* there, and meet me fairly, now show thy Valour, and preserve thy Life, by taking mine; for all the Powers above have joyn'd consent, that one of us must fall'.

Turgesius could no longer listen to his threats, but (disengaging himself from *Dooneflaith*, he cry'd out) 'Good Gods, if Insolence like this, to me, who am thy King, shall 'scape without its just Reward, and go away unpunish'd, let every Schoolboy whip me with a Rod; and may the Women brand me, with the hated Name of Coward! Die Traytor (goes he on making a stroak at him) since one of us must fall, take a Death too glorious for so base a Villain from thy Monarch's Hands'.

Here they both engag'd in Fight, but *Dooneflaith* fearing the loss of her lov'd *Murchoe*, catches hold of *Turgesius*'s Arms, by which means she gave *Murchoe* opportunity to get within him, and disarm him. 'Now, Sir (says *Murchoe*) but that I scorn so poor and base Revenge, and would not use the advantage given me by a Woman, I'd ease the Kingdom of its Thraldome, and free my self from a perfidious Rival. 'Tis she alone, that vertuous lovely Lady, whose presence charms my Hand from giving thee that Death which thou deservest. O Madam (says he turning to *Dooneflaith*) how inglorious have you made my Name! that, had you given me leave, might have resounded through the World, and born the Title of its Countrys Saver! *Ireland* should then have had its native Liberty again, and I perhaps been chose their King, proud only in that Glory, to lay my Crown beneath your Feet'.

Turgesius (with a dauntless Front) told him how much he was indebted to *Dooneflaith*, who had not only Repeal'd his Banishment, but had now given him the advantage over him. He told him withal, how base and mean insulting was; and bid him, since he was in his power, to use him as he pleas'd; but charg'd him still to be mindful how he got the Victory so much he boasted of. *Murchoe* cou'd no longer endure the thoughts of making use of the Advantage given him against a single Man, threw *Turgesius* his Sword, and bid him use it once more. But *Dooneflaith* ran to him, and with Tears in her Eyes, besought him to desist; but nothing could prevail; and had not some of the Courtiers and Guards (who by this time were come to the place, hearing the clashing of Swords) prevented (by disarming the valiant *Murchoe*) *Turgesius* had a second time fall'n under his Mercy; for just as they had seiz'd on him, *Turgesius*'s Sword broke short to his Hand.

It was not without many commands that *Turgesius* himself cou'd hinder the enrag'd Soldiers from taking *Murchoe*'s Life, and cutting him to pieces even before his Mistresses Eyes, who now pleaded in his behalf so persuasively, that she obtain'd of the Monarch his Liberty of Life, with Condition that he forthwith left the Kingdom. *Murchoe* after what he had done, was glad at present on any Conditions to get from the malice of the enraged *Danes*; wherefore without so much as taking his Leave of *Dooneflaith*, he fled from the Court; but not being willing to leave his Native Soil, by which he knew he should utterly be depriv'd of all means of serving his Mistress; whose absence now ran more in his Mind than all his other Misfortunes, his Life became in two or three Days so cumbersom to him, that he was resolv'd either to lose it, or free it, together with all *Ireland* of the Tyrannous Burthen it bore. To which end, he posts to *Armagh*,* whereof *Turgesius* was quickly inform'd, and at four several times in one Month, caused Fire to be set to that City, to drive him from thence: Nor did he spare either Monastery or Church that stood in his way, lest he should take Sanctuary in them. He likewise put to Death all their Priests, and plac'd Heathen Lay-Abbots in every Cloister. Nor did his fury spare either Sex or Age, whom he thought favour'd his Concealment.

The poor afflicted *Dooneflaith* spent all her Nights and Days in most cruel condolement for the loss of her *Murchoe*; nor could all the fair Promises or large Offers *Turgesius* could make, win her to bestow on him, even to his own Face, any other than the Title of Tyrant; in hopes that thereby she might raise his Cruelty to that pitch, as to give her a Death, which next to the Love of her dear *Murchoe*, would now be most welcome unto her.

Turgesius's Love now became so fierce and unruly in his Breast, that nothing but the Enjoyment of *Dooneflaith* could allay it, or give him one moment of ease; he resolv'd in himself, nothing should *impede* his Desires; wherefore he once more sends to her Father *Maolseachelvin*, to use his Authority with his Daughter, and make her more pliant to his Love; or that all who belong'd to her, should feel the weight of his Anger, and know how fatal the Consequence should be in case she refus'd, and did not come willingly into his Arms; he had left off his Addresses to her, after having found her impregnable, and waited a while for an Answer from *Maolseachelvin*.

Some days pass'd, and the unfortunate *Dooneflaith* began to entertain hopes that the Tyrant had quitted his Suit, and that her ill usage of him had banish'd his Love; she had now time enough to bewail her Misfortunes, and miss'd not a Day, in which she went not to the Grove in the Garden to ease her sorrowful Heart by Complaints. One Day among the rest, she was got into an Arbour, where having wearied her self with her Grief, soft slumbers seal'd up her Eyes, and laid her to Sleep, and in her Dreams she imagin'd she saw *Murchoe* all bloody come into her Room, and give her a thousand Reproaches of being unfaithful; then pulling a Sword from under his Robe, he would have pierc'd his own Breast; at the sight whereof, *Dooneflaith* started out of her Sleep, in such an Agony, that she was not her self in an hour or two after. But having well consider'd 'twas only a Dream, and the Fancy of her Distemper'd Brain, she fell to complaining again.

'Oh! merciless Powers, said she, how long will you make me the Mark of your Anger? why, O relentless Heav'ns! are you so Cruel! Oh ease me of my Misery, or Life! For what unknown Offence do you afflict me thus? Thus Rack and Torture one, who always to the utmost of her Power, has been Obedient to your holy Wills! which even now, amidst this Mass of Woe, I willingly submit unto! All I request, is but one farewell sight of him I love next to yourselves; let him but once more bless my Eyes, and I shall die contented'.

No sooner had she utter'd these words, but she saw at the entrance of the Arbour, one in a Womans Dress, who at first view she knew not; but recollecting her self, she perceiv'd to be *Murchoe*. 'Thanks, bounteous Heaven, said she, now my Prayers are heard, this Charitable Act has cancell'd all your former Cruelty; wellcome my Love', says she, running to take him in her Arms; but how was she surpriz'd to see him shun her soft Embraces! and stood gazing on her, as tho' he had never seen her before. 'Ah! *Murchoe*, says the charming Maid, is it thus you requite all my Sufferings? Can my Embraces be thought troublesome! or sure I do mistake, and this is not my Love, but some illusion that does wear his Face, and come to mock my Miseries'.

Murchoe was so astonish'd at his suddain* Happiness, that he could scarcely believe what he heard, or saw; and *Dooneflaith* was so much alter'd with her continual Pineing and Grief, that he scarce knew her: But his Senses assuming their former strength, he ran to her, and fell at her feet, where he vented such a flood of Tears, and so many Sighs, that he was not able for some time to utter one word, while the passionate *Dooneflaith*, fearing he was grown unkind, or jealous, fell down by him in a Trance.

Murchoe, not minding where he was, and what hazard he ran of discovering himself, and consequently of losing his Life, call'd out for Help, naming himself a thousand times over, to have been the unfortunate fatal Cause.

'Oh! *Murchoe*, *Murchoe*, said he, what hast thou done? Oh! I cou'd stab my Heart, tear all my Limbs, and gnaw my very Flesh, for being thus rash! Cursed be my Life, and blasted be my Hopes, which thus have made me take on this Disguise, O *Dooneflaith*, my lovely Dear, my charming Saint look up, look up, thy *Murchoe* calls; more miserable now than are the wretched Damn'd! Oh ye Inhabitants above, look down, and lend your aid; recall the parting Life of her whose Loss will make this Kingdom Poor'.

Dooneflaith by this time coming to her self again, gave him a Sign that she liv'd by a Groan. 'O blessed sound, said he, what Musick dost thou make in my Heart! such a sad accent coming from my Love, at any other time, wou'd rend my very Soul; but now since 'tis the Messenger of Life, 'tis more Melodious than the Songs of Angels are; repeat it once again, and bless my Ears'.–'Ha! says *Dooneflaith*, where am I? What super-Officious Hand hath brought me back to Life! What more than savage Beast, could be so cruel to awake me from my long Eternal Sleep'. But opening her Eyes and seeing *Murchoe*, she alter'd her Note, and gave Heav'n a thousand thanks for their Kindness, and ask'd him forgiveness for what she had said.

He had yet no power to Answer, nor wou'd his Kisses permit her to finish what e'er she began, and to their mutual Content and Satisfaction, they spent some time in the silent Oratory of their Eyes, where each so feelingly did tell such

Stories, as Words cou'd ne'er express. *Murchoe* was the first who broke silence, and return'd her a million of Thanks for the interest she had taken in all that he suffer'd, they made a thousand new Protestations of Loving till Death, and gave each other firm assurances of future Fidelity. They were parting, with Promises to see each other as often as they could when *Maolseachelvin* her Father enters, taking *Murchoe*, (not minding his Face, which he took care to conceal,) for one of his Daughters Women, let him pass by without the least suspicion.

Maolseachelvin told *Dooneflaith* that she must prepare, for in three Days he had promis'd *Turgesius* to send her unto him, accompany'd with fifteen other Virgins, as a Victim to allay the Fury, that her Obstinacy, and *Murchoe*'s Treachery had rais'd in his Breast. He stay'd not to receive any Answer, but went forwards to perfect the Walk he intended, and to think of the Project that was working in his Brain.

No sooner was he out of sight, but the afflicted *Dooneflaith* betook her to the Arbour again, and throwing her self on a Bank, she vented her Sorrow in this manner. 'Oh Cruel, Barbarous Father, said she, and have you at length consented to a separation 'twixt me, and my *Murchoe*, to become the Wife of *Turgesius*. But that, I can easily hinder. Besides, he has Sworn he will never Request it, but by my permission, which I will sooner grant to Furies to hurry me to Hell. No, inhuman Parent, tho' you and all the World wou'd grant me His! yet if none else will, Death shall forbid the Banes.* But if forgetful of his Oaths, he forces me to Wed him, ev'n in the Tyrant's sight, I'll Pierce my Heart, and spurt the reaking* stream full in his hated Face'.

Murchoe having seen *Maolseachelvin* quit his Daughter, and observing her to retire back into the Arbour, follow'd after her, to enquire what her Father had said. But in what a Consternation was he? when, as he entred, he beheld her tearing her lovely Hair, and imprinting the marks of her Rage on her beautiful Face, and giving such stroaks on her tender Breast, as were enough to force Life from its seat. *Murchoe* ran to her, and put a stop to her Hands, which surely else had ruin'd so much Beauty, as none but she could ever boast of. 'Oh! unkind *Dooneflaith*, said he to her, what new affliction has befall'n my Love? that thus she seeks to spoil the fairest Temple, Beauty ever fram'd'. 'Oh *Murchoe*, replies the despairing *Dooneflaith*, leave me to my self, my Griefs are catching, and with its black Contagion will infect thy Soul; Heaven has not yet left pouring down its Wrath, and what alone was meant for me, may fall on you; the Gods above have mark'd me out a Subject for their utmost Cruelties! My Father,—Oh, I blush to call him so, forgetting me, forgetting Honour and himself, has giv'n me o'er into the Tyrant's Hands; but Three Days time I have allow'd to mourn the loss of thee my Love, and everlasting Happiness'.

'How short, says *Murchoe*, and fading are poor Lover's Joys? For but some Moments since, I thought my self in Heaven, and whilst infolded in my *Dooneflaith*'s Arms, I thought no Misery cou'd e'er approach me! Then what a Fall is here, flung down at once from that stupendous height, and dash'd in pieces in the lowest Hell. Oh *Maolseachelvin*, whither is all thy Glory fled? How canst thou condescend to give this Gem to one who knows not half the value of it'.

While they were thus condoling their hard fortune, and saying all the soft things Love could inspire them with, *Maolseachelvin* returns, and hearing his Daughter's Voice in the Arbour, enter'd, and found our Lovers Arm in Arm, in which posture they had resolv'd to end their Lives together, and never part, but go Hand in Hand to Death: Which had not her Father entred, and snatch'd the Dagger out of *Murchoe*'s Hands, had been effected.

Murchoe seeing *Maolseachelvin*, could not forbear discovering himself to him, and giving him a thousand Reproaches for yielding to the Tyrant's will. *Maolseachelvin* was amaz'd to find him in Company with his Daughter, and in such a Dress; but having resolv'd with himself what to do, he thought it but Wisdom to conceal it till some fitter Season. Wherefore not minding what *Murchoe* said to him, he ask'd his Daughter, if she had consider'd well of what he had told her.

'Most Honour'd Sir, reply'd the weeping *Dooneflaith*, can I admit such Thoughts as those; your self, nay Heav'n must Curse me if I do! What, Wed a Tyrant! one whose wicked Hands have ransack'd all our Holy Temples, demolish'd all our Altars! burnt all our Churches, and raz'd our Monasteries, Ravish'd our Nuns, slain our Pious Priests, and thrown the very Sacred Host it self to the Dogs; whose Tyranny has Murder'd our Nobles, and fir'd our Towns and Cities! Can such an one be thought a Match for her, whom you with Pious Care have taught to hate! Oh! rather, Sir, (upon my Knees I beg it) take back this wretched Life you once bestow'd me'.

'No, Daughter, answers *Maolseachelvin*, 'tis not to be his Wife (for that's a Name which blasts the Lover's Joys) he'd have you only for his Concubine, use you a while, and then return you back, you have taken Care he ne'er shall be your Husband, by the Oaths you've made him swear, and in Revenge, he is resolv'd to have you – his Mistress'. Reply'd *Dooneflaith* hastily, 'Oh! Heavens, my Father sure is Mad; his Reverend Heart o'er-laden with its Fears, has banish'd Sense from thence! What, be the Tyrant's Mistress! You cannot sure have such a thought as that! you say but this to try my Resolution! O, have some pity on your wretched Daughter, add not more misery unto my troubled Breast, already overburden'd with my Woes'.

Maolseachelvin could hardly refrain from Tears, to see the sad Condition his Daughter was in; however he goes on, and laid before her the Power of *Turgesius*, and that if she did not willingly consent, he would have her by force. 'Think, says he to her, how you cou'd endure to see a loving Father Murder'd before your Face; for that and more he swears to do, if you consent not to his Love; he vows when he has had his Will, which all the Powers above he is resolv'd shall not hinder, he'll give your Body to the vilest *Danes*, and let the meanest Soldiers use you as they please. Then think again, how happy thou may'st live, how High and Glorious sit on *Ireland*'s Throne, if by your Love you sooth this Mighty Monarch'.

Murchoe who all this while stood Thunder-struck to hear these impious urgings of her Father, cou'd no longer forbear uttering his Mind, with Eyes sparkling with Anger, he stept up to him. 'And can *Maolseachelvin*, says he, then become so base? Can he, whom *Ireland*'s Hopes are fix'd upon, degenerate from his Vertuous Noble Ancestors, and from a Prince, become a Bawd! unheard of Wickedness, a Pander* to his Child! 'Twill cancel all my former thoughts of Vertue, and make me think thou never didst beget her; for surely such a pure untainted stream cou'd never rise from so impure a Spring! Or were you ten times over her Father, if it were possible, she shou'd not now obey; I with these Hands wou'd sooner give her Death my self'.

'No, Ambitious, Vain-glorious Boy, answers *Maolseachelvin*, it is not in thy Power to give her Death, or save thy Life'– So calling to two young Gentlemen, who waited without, and whom he had won to his Purpose, and had promis'd in all things to follow his Directions, he commanded them to lay hold on *Murchoe*, and then went on. 'Now see rash Youth, says he, how Fatal 'tis to play with Thunder, whose Bolt has fallen, and crush'd thee to the Earth; I'll send thee bound in Chains along with her, which Act will doubly gain *Turgesius*'s Heart'.

Dooneflaith seeing them seize on *Murchoe*, ran to him, and taking hold of his Arms, would have stop'd him; but her Father loosing her hold, she fell upon her Knees, and, with a Torrent of Tears, besought him to save the Life of *Murchoe*. 'Do with me, says she, what you please, give my unspotted Honour to the Tyrant's Lust, Brand me with Infamy, but save this Noble Youth'.

'Yes, Mistress, answers her Father, your Honour is unspotted, when in your Arms I found the lusty Lover; for thy sake only, tis he now shall die'. 'O Good Gods! (cries out *Dooneflaith*) where shall the Innocent fly for Refuge, if you neglect protecting them? Am I the wretched Cause that he must bleed? Oh! Heavens, I thought it was not in your Power to add, to what I felt before; but now my misery is doubled on me. Oh! dearest Father have you quite forgot all pity, abandon'd all remorse? Can you suspect me guilty of so foul a Crime, and let me breath? I that till now you always counted good! Witness ye all-knowing Powers how guiltless I am of this blasting Calumny; by all that's Holy, Just and Sacred

> *No Lustful Heat e'er warm'd my Virgin Breast;*
> *Bate but that Thought, and I'll forgive the rest.**

Then look upon his Youth, his hopeful, Noble Youth, and pity his Misfortunes; he knows no Sin, unless vertuous Love be such. O dearest Father, I conjure you save his Life, by all the Charms which Honour can inspire; by my dear Mothers Soul, by all your hopes of *Ireland*'s Future Happiness, and by the Glory you shall win by this good Deed, release him strait, let not me beg in vain, you was not us'd to see me thus in Tears upon my Knees, and yet refuse to grant me my Request'.

Murchoe seeing *Maolseachelvin* so obdurate to all her Intreaties, fell likewise on his Knees. 'Behold, said he, with Tears, the humble *Murchoe* suppliant at thy Feet, who begs not to preserve his Life, but your dear Daughter's Honour, send her away, and lay the blame on me, I'll own 'twas I, who bore her from his Arms; then to appease his Wrath, let me be sent unto him, I'll willingly endure his utmost rage, and count my Life well spent to save her Virtue'.

'Oh! no, dear honour'd Sir, says *Dooneflaith*, first send me to his Arms, where you will only lose a Woman's Life, my Vertue cannot suffer so long as there are means to stop my breath; or when the Letcher comes all fir'd with Lust, I'll cool his Veins, by letting forth his blood, or at the worst, I'll drown him in my own'.

Maolseachelvin could no longer hold out; but running first to his Daughter, then doing the like to *Murchoe*, he took them both into his Arms, and wept a flood upon their Necks. 'Right virtuous Pair, said he, whom Heaven has sent to make me happy in my latter days, my loving Children both; forgive the Tryal I have made; Now witness for me all ye bless'd above, I hold ye equally as dear as Life, as Honour, or my precious Soul; and since I find so well you Love each other, curs'd be that Man who would untie this Knot: Now wipe your Tears away as I do mine, tho' sprung from different Causes; yours, from your Sorrows, mine, from mighty Joy; stifle your Grief, as I conceal my Vengeance. Make thee his Mistress——Now Heaven forgive me, if I would not sooner damn than harbour such a thought; I for my dear lov'd Daughter's honour, would set at nought my sweet immortal Soul. No, *Dooneflaith*, no, Generous *Murchoe*, I have so contriv'd it, she shall be sent to him, and as he writes to me here (shewing them the Letter willingly,) has also commanded me to send him Fifteen young Virgins of our Noblest Blood, to slake the burning lust of his Chief

Officers, I'll send them too. But since so well thy Womans Dress becomes thee, thou shalt be one, and Fourteen Youths,* as Bold and Valiant as thy self shall go, all clad and dress'd like thee, with each a Sword beneath their Gowns. I have sent to those who have taken shelter in the Woods, Mountains, and Boggs, to be in readiness, and have a Thousand Men, who at the Signal given, shall fall upon his Guards. Letters already I have dispatch'd to every City in our Country, to bid them Rise on such a Night'.

'When you are entred, and they all deep in Wine, frolick and gay, their Bloods all boyling hot, secure each one his Officer by Death, I'll trust my Daughter with the Tyrant's Fate; strike home my Girl, and dip thy Dagger to the Hilt, then let him take his fill of Love, Caress and Court thee then. But now we must disperse; and you, *Murchoe* till after to Morrow, which is the appointed Day, shall lie conceal'd in my House; these Gentlemen who are my trusty Countrymen, and well approved Friends, shall forthwith to the scatter'd *Irish*, and get 'em to an Head, then lead them like a Torrent on our Foes'.

They all swore Secrecy, and departed, only *Dooneflaith* and *Murchoe* were not separated till it was late, but went together into her Chamber, where, to their inexpressible satisfaction and mutual joy, they Supp'd together, and passed away the hours till Bedtime, then *Murchoe* was Conducted into an Apartment by himself, where he spent that Night on the thoughts of the past Days Adventures, and the important Affairs they were to perform in a short time after.

The next Morning *Maolseachelvin* sent a Messenger to *Turgesius*, promising according to his Commands, that he had won on his Daughter to obey him; and that as he hop'd for his Kingly Favour hereafter, he would not fail upon the Morrow Night to send her, accompany'd with Fifteen Virgins more, who were also willing to run the same Fate, and participate of the Joys their Mistress should receive in so splendid an Entertainment.

Turgesius was almost ravish'd with this News, for certainly no Man ever lov'd, or rather lusted to the degree he did; he was resolv'd to have lost the whole Kingdom but he would enjoy her; his eager Joy sat heavy on his Heart, for Love is most impatient on Crown'd Heads. But finding her come thus easily, he spar'd not for any thing that might make her Reception Magnificent. He sent for Fifteen of his Chiefest Commanders, and told them what a Treatment* he had for them. In short, the whole Court was almost new model'd, the Rooms adorn'd with Rich Beds, and the most Costly Hangings.

Never was Palace so galantly set out with Gold, Jewels, and Tapestry as this, not any thing below the Dignity of Silver, and that curiously wrought and Massive, was us'd in any of the Chambers; Cloth of Tissue was the meanest Furniture they had; the Candlesticks were Gold; so that all the Wealth those Sacrilegious *Danish* Heathens had despoil'd the Churches and Monasteries of, with all the Plunder they had taken at Sacking of Towns, and King's Courts, were all now brought to this Palace; so that it might be said, That one Spot of Ground, held more Wealth than all *Ireland* besides.

Nor were the Wines but of the Richest, and all the variety of Viands which could be procur'd, were sent for to this Place, and every one was employ'd in some Office or other; and the King, with his Commanders almost Mad for the arrival of the happy Night, their longing impatience thought that almost an Age, which was only but twenty four Hours.

The Hour at length arriv'd, and *Dooneflaith* set out with a Noble Train of suppos'd young Virgins, whereof Fifteen of them were of the most Handsome, and yet most Stout and Resolute Youths of *Ireland*, as well and gloriously Dress'd as

Hands, Jewels, and Art could effect it; each having one or two others to attend him as his Servant, or Waiting-Woman, in the same Female Apparel, and each a short Sword under his Gown.

Turgesius went about a Mile out of his Court to meet them, as soon as he had news of their approach, accompanied with Fifteen of his Choicest Commanders, some whereof he had sent for out of strong Cities wherein they Commanded, who also had with them an equal Train of Attendants.

The first interview of the two Parties, was such a Sight as might have equal'd, if not exceeded, that of *Alexander*, when he met *Thalestris* and her *Amazons* upon the Banks of the *Euphrates*.*

It seem'd as tho' *Mars** himself had led the Van of all the other Gods, to meet with *Venus** and the Female Deities.

Turgesius, and all who follow'd him, quite forgetting their Grandeur, and Martial Habitude, descended from their shining Gilded Chariots, and went to those of the Ladies. Nor had *Maolseachelvin* spar'd Cost to make his Daughters Equipage more Magnificent and Glorious than any that *Ireland* had seen before, especially that of the Charming *Dooneflaith*, which was so Richly Furnish'd, that at a distance in the glittering Sun-beams it was too Glorious to be lookt upon, and struck a sort of Blindness in the Spectator's Eyes who beheld it. She was drawn by six milk white Horses, Caparison'd with Trappings of Gold, and the Chariot wherein she rode was open, having Rich Embroider'd Curtains held up by young *Cupids*, who seem'd well pleas'd, and smiling at the Deity that they attended; nor were the others much less sumptuous.

In short, who e're had been to see the first Greeting, could not but have been astonish'd at so Noble a Sight. *Turgesius*, (as tho' he had long practis'd the Art of Love) so behav'd himself, that even *Dooneflaith* was mov'd with Compassion, at the great Action she was to perform. However, she seem'd as eager to receive his Caresses, as if she had met with the Man whom her Soul ador'd. After some few Compliments had pass'd on either side, (the Women having by this time alighted to meet the Men) they all mounted again, the Monarch taking *Dooneflaith* into his own Chariot, and the other Commanders following his Example, did the like with those who came with her.

And now being Pair'd, they set forward for the Court; all the way that they rode, they were diverted by Trumpets and Wind-Musick, which in their turns made a Seraphick Harmony. But that which most of all Charm'd the Ears of the Warriours, were the soft and melting Expressions the counterfeit Ladies did use; which were so ravishing, and tender, that not one of *Turgesius*'s Train but could willingly have wish'd to have pass'd by the Ceremony of Supping, and have gone immediately to their Chambers; even *Turgesius* himself thought the time, tho' spent in his Mistresses Company but irksom and long, so eager was he to have the sweet Charmer in his Embraces.

But Supper being ended, the description whereof, would but delay the recital of things more material, they prepar'd for their Beds, and *Dooneflaith* was led up by the suppos'd Maidens who came with her to the Chamber that was assign'd for the Monarch; He being impatient for the dear happiness his Soul so much long'd for, thought them too tedious in undressing her, and putting her to Bed; being no longer able to defer the happy moment, disarm'd himself below, as all the rest of the Commanders did, laying their Arms on a Table in the great Hall, went each to his Chamber, expecting the coming of Her he had chose. But *Turgesius* no sooner entred his Room, for he came alone, than he was seiz'd on, and immediately gagg'd, that no out-cry might be made; they had certainly kill'd him, had not *Murchoe* interceeded; who told him he now paid him back a Debt that he ow'd him, ever since he was so generous to save his Life formerly from the outrage of his Soldiers and Guards, who were ready to have cut him in pieces, when he fought with him in *Dooneflaith*'s Apartment; in retaliation of which, he wou'd now save his Life from the threatning Swords of those who justly thirsted for his Blood.

Turgesius was not a little surpriz'd at the unlook'd for Adventure; but above all, at the gallant Generosity of his Noble Enemy, and incens'd Rival, he would have made him such an Answer as suited the greatness of the Act, had he had the liberty of speaking. But now his Heart was so troubled at the loss of *Dooneflaith*, and all his ravishing hopes were so blasted, that Life to him was but an unnecessary thing; he began tho' too late, to think how dearly he must pay for his Lust, and how pompous the Solemnity had been made for the bringing on his utter Destruction.

The thoughts of the loss of a Crown, came crowding upon him, and he could not but be sensible what a lasting Infamy this Action must lay on his blind and inconsiderate Credulity. How would he, in his Mind, Curse the time that he first saw that Charming Seducer, and now beheld her with more Detestation and Horror, than heretofore he had done with Love and Pleasure.

But we must leave him to himself, and return to the rest, who (after the seizing *Turgesius*) had no better success than their King, unless ending a miserable Life might be accounted some mitigation of their Misfortunes. The Signal was presently given out of the Court Windows to the small Army that *Maolseachelvin* had brought to the Gates, and all those Attendants and Servants who came with his Daughter, were in a readiness to give the Onset to those in the Palace.

Turgesius and his Train no sooner rose from the Table, but the inferior Commanders and Officers were set down to it; each with one of those under Women who came with *Dooneflaith*; the Bowls of Wine were going merrily about, and the *Danes* (who are potent in *Bacchus*'s Battles)* were too busie, and the Musick too loud to let them hear *Maolseachelvin*, when with his Arm'd Men he forc'd his way into the Palace; and they were greatly surpriz'd when they saw a whole Band of stout *Irish-men* well Arm'd enter the Hall. It was now no time to demand what they meant; for e'er they could scarce turn about to see who they were, they met with their Fate.

A greater Confusion was never seen, the Tables were all overthrown, and the Blood of the *Danes*, with that of the Grape, promiscuously mingled, made a purple Deluge on the Floor; nor was there a *Dane* that Night in the Court, who found not his Death, except *Turgesius* the Tyrant, who was reserv'd for a more ignominious and miserable End.

Nor had this Great Undertaking any worse success in the other parts of *Ireland*; for those Towns and Cities whose Governours were slain at the Feast (more bloody than that of the *Centaurs*)* hearing of the loss of their Commanders and their King, lost with them their Courage, and yielded an easie Victory to the brave *Irish*, who in a short time after, releas'd the whole Kingdom from the slavish Tyranny of the *Danes*, to their Lawful Subjection under a Monarch of their own, which was by the consent of the Nobles plac'd on *Maolseachelvin*, for the gallant Exploit he had done, for then their Monarchs were Elective, and with good reason the Choice fell on him.

Now the *Irish* had thrown off the *Danish* Yoak, and were again at Liberty, each enjoying the benefit of Peace, which was introduc'd by a most bloody and furious War. Nor was there a *Dane* left in the whole Country, but such who they us'd as their Slaves, and put to mean Offices; and those who were before so busie in demolishing and burning of Churches and Monasteries, were now employ'd either as Smiths, Carpenters, or Masons, in their Re-building, and the Church-Lands were all restor'd to their proper uses. The Lay-Abbots whom the *Danes* had plac'd there, were cast out of the Cloisters and slain, and the whole Kingdom began once more to Flourish in Christianity, and was establish'd in the true Worship of God.

It is necessary, e'er we proceed any farther, to give a step back, and see what became of our Lovers, and the depos'd Usurper; who, some time after his Defeat, was led about the Streets, thro' which so often he had rode in Splendor and Triumph, now Manacled, and loaden with Chains, and became a scoff and derision to those, o'er whom so lately he Triumph'd, and in this Condition (with a shouting throng of the Vulgar) was he conducted to the River *Laugh-Ainme*,* into which he was cast, and finish'd a burthensom Life, by being there drowned.

Our two Lovers, had now, as they thought, no other Obstacle, but the consent of *Bryan Boriamh*e Father to *Murchoe*, who they hop'd would agree to their Marriage. The Valiant *Murchoe* in that Night's great Action, having shifted his Womans Apparel, put on the more becoming one of Arms, and flew like Lightning to assist his Country-men, leaving the care and safeguard of *Dooneflaith* to her Father, and it was some days e'er he return'd, but to his great misery; for now *Maolseachelvin* having the prospect of a Crown in his sight, and having stomach'd *Bryan*'s denial of their Marriage before, was firmly resolv'd that interest should not bring him to consent to it now. Wherefore going to his Daughter, and taking her into his Closet, he Commanded her on her Duty, no longer to think of her Lover; but when *Murchoe* return'd, to use him as one who was most indiffer-ent to her.

'Oh! dearest Sir, says *Dooneflaith*, can what you say be true? Can he who sav'd my Honour, and redeem'd his mourning Country be thus hardly us'd by me!' 'He save thy Honour, and redeem his Country (replies her Father in an angry tone) did you your self, did I, and all the rest of the brave Princes of this Land, do nothing? Hear what I say, and for your life obey me, for what I have design'd, no Prayers, or Charms, tho' drest in the best Garb of Eloquence, adorn'd with all the Tears and taking Looks thy Beauty can put on, tho' on thy Knees thou follow'st me about, thou shalt not shake or move my fixt resolve. If when *Murchoe* shall return, with eager Joys to run into thine Arms, with frowns and scorns avoid his soft Embraces, give him no Answer, but disdainful Looks, or here I swear I'll stab him before thy Face'.

'Oh! Reverend Sir, says *Dooneflaith*, recal that cruel Oath; how can you think this Heart, that is all Love, all soft and tender to the noble *Murchoe*, can teach my Face to put on such disguise! Cou'd I consent, to shew my Filial Duty, and obey, my Eyes would soon betray my Heart; and tho' my words were cold and all unkind, yet they would shoot such fiery Darts, as would declare they were but counterfeit; my very Eyes, spight of my best efforts, would talk and tell the tenders of my Soul; each interrupting sigh I give, will bear no consort with my Tongue'.

'By Heaven (says her Father) do as I command, shew but one amorous glance, one heave, one pant, or sigh, and I will blind those tell-tale Eyes of thine, and give thee truly cause to sigh, by giving him his Death'. 'Sure, Sir (replies the weeping *Dooneflaith*) you cannot mean the thing you speak! You say it but to try my Love a second time; which by the Gods is still the same it was, when in the Garden you made the former Test'. 'No, Minion,* says *Maolseachelvin*, I do it not to try thy Love, which I'm too sensible is true; I do it to revenge his

Father's Scorn, who would not give consent that he should Wed thee when I was a private Man, nor shall he now I'm King; therefore once more observe what I command'.

'And must the innocent *Murchoe*, says she, who always dearly lov'd me, and sought not Heaven with more earnest Prayers than he sought me, be punish'd thus for his unkind Father's Fault? Oh! Sir, reverse your cruel Doom,* if not for his sake, yet for mine, nay for your own; for if I share an interest in your Heart, 'twill grieve you sure to see your only Daughter die, when with one word you may preserve her Life. What! quit my Love, now after this Misery and Trouble we have pass'd through for it! now grow unkind, when he most merits Love! and after all those Sacred Oaths and Vows, those thousand Protestations, which even in your hearing, I have made to Love him ever, now to re-call that sacred Breath, and hurl damnation on my perjur'd Soul'.

'I ask you not, says he, to break your Vows; but meet him as I now command you, that his proud Father may be humbled, and fall a low Petitioner for the Love he once rejected'.

'A thousand Blessings sit upon your Head, says she, and make your Crown more glorious than all your Predecessors were, those healing words have cur'd my bleeding heart; now I will call you dear and loving Father, kneel and adore the very ground you go on; use what severity you please against his Father, but let my *Murchoe* not be put in pain; let me not see him rather, till his suppliant Father begs your pardon; for certainly to see him as you bid me, will prove so fatal, that twill break his Heart'.

'Trifle no more (replies *Maolseachelvin*) but punctually obey my will, I see them yonder entring the Court; and once more swear, if that you fail in any Point I have enjoyn'd you, you ne'er shall meet him more, but in the Grave'.

After this he left her, and went to his own Chamber; no sooner was he parted, but *Dooneflaith* looking out at the Window, beheld her dear *Murchoe*, with his Father just entring the Palace; and not being able to think on the severe Injunctions her Father had laid on her, without a torrent of Tears, and a thousand imprecations on her unkind Stars. 'O barbarous Father, said she to her self, more Tyrannous and Cruel to thy Child, than Savage Monsters are to those they hate; not see my Love, but with disdainful looks! not give him one kind glance for all his Love! not one kind word of thanks for all his pains! this Cruelty exceeds all precedent! my unkind Speech or Eyes will do the fatal Work, and leave no business for my Father's Sword! O that some Angel would instruct my Love, and tell him that my Eyes and Tongue are Lyars, that my poor Heart bears no consent to what they say; tell him I am all over Love, and that my *Murchoe* is more precious to my Soul than all the World besides'.

Murchoe, and his Father, with several of his Friends were now come into the outward Court of the Palace, and casting his Eyes up to the Window, he beheld his adorable Mistress; who no sooner saw him, but withdrew from the Place, which *Murchoe* thought was done to haste to him. 'Oh! Father (says he, almost Extasied) look how the Treasure of my Soul does fly to meet my longing Arms; now all the Blood I've lost in *Ireland*'s Wars, will largely be Rewarded'.

Bryan took such part in his Sons Transports, that he could hardly forbear shedding Tears of Joy. But *Murchoe* lest he should be out-done in kindness, made what hast he cou'd into the House, and at the end of the Hall beheld his fair *Dooneflaith*, whom he ran unto with all the speed his Love could make. 'Oh! thou charming, soft and lovely Maid, said the transported *Murchoe*, let me upon thy tender Breast breath the soft languishments of my o'er flowing Joy'! But how did he start, and look amaz'd, when he not only saw she met him not half way, but shun'd his Arms; and after a small pause, with gazing Eyes he thus went on.

'What, my *Dooneflaith*, says he, are my Embraces loathsom grown! What, dost thou turn away the warming Sunshine of thine Eyes; not one kind look to crown thy *Murchoe*'s Victory, not one soft word to bid him wellcome home!' *Dooneflaith* could no longer turn away her Head, yet was afraid of her Father, who through a secret place look'd into the Hall, and beheld her with frowns; and fearing she should not perform what he bid her, her Love and she must part for ever; cast so disdainful and scornful a look upon *Murchoe*, that he clapping his Hand to his Heart, cry'd out, 'O Gods! those cruel piercing Eyes have stab'd my Soul, and given me a death my boldest Enemies could never do'. Then after a little stop, he went up to her, and would have taken her by the Hand, but she refus'd it him; telling him the unkindness of her Father had destroy'd their Loves, and that now he had fallen from his Promise, and had commanded her no more to look on him with Amorous Eyes; in pursuance to whose will, she did from thence forward forbid him to visit her.

Murchoe, during her talk stood like one without Motion, nor had he the power to utter one word, till he saw her departing the Hall; but then running 'twixt her and the Door, he fell on his Knees, and beg'd her for her former Love to hear his latest words; but she overcome with the pitiful sight, being no longer able to look on one in that woful Condition, and one whom contrary to her will, she her self had made so, return'd him no Answer; but snatching her Hand out of his, which e'er she was aware he had seiz'd, without so much as looking back, she went out of the Hall, and left the Disconsolate *Murchoe* on his Knees.

He continu'd in that posture till she was gone out of sight; then rising on his Legs again, he drew forth his Sword, and had ended his Life on its Point, had not his Father, and Friends (who expected no less) stept in and prevented him. 'Oh! Cruel Father, say he to *Bryan*, this last unkindness, outdoes all you have done to me before; why would you have me live, when Life's so great a burden? Were it not better I at once gave up my breath, than live in lingring pain, and deal it out by sighs! O Faithless Woman, says he a little after, thou abstract of Inconstancy, where's now that charming Voice which with kind Protestations swore, *Murchoe* should ever be her Souls delight; farewell, a long and last farewell, for with your cold disdain you've blasted all my Hopes, and now no remedy is left but Death'.

With much ado at last, they got him home to his Chamber, but twas not in their power to get him to Eat, or take the least refreshment; and it was a long time before his Father could get him to promise to use no violence on himself; to which he would never have consented, had not *Bryan* told him, he would use all his Endeavour to alter *Maolseachelvin*'s Resolutions.

No sooner was his Father gone out of the Room, but he commanded all who were with him to do the like; and after two or three hasty turns in the Chamber, he flung himself on his Bed, where he pour'd out such Tears, such Sighs, and Complaints, that he drew moisture from the Eyes of all who look'd in at the Keyhole of the Door to see what he did. But now let us return again to our History.

Soon after all things were settled in Peace, the Victorious *Maolseachelvin*, was as is said before, by the Election of the Princes and Nobility of *Ireland*,* deservedly made King of *Meath*, and then Monarch of the whole Country; when there arriv'd three Brothers out of *Norway*, viz. *Amelanus*, *Cytaracus*, and *Ivorus*,* with their Families, and great Trains, who (in a most Amicable and Peaceable manner) pretending to be Merchants, obtain'd leave for the better carrying on their Traffick and Trade, to build three Cities near the Sea side; which was permitted them, upon Condition, that they paid Tribute for them. Articles of Agreement being consented too, on both sides, they fell to Work, and erected the three Cities, now call'd *Dublin*, *Waterford*, and *Limrick*; which they had no sooner finished, and had made almost impregnable by strong Fortifications, but the *Irish* began to see their Error, and now it was that they felt the Power of an Enemy, no less prejudicial in all appearance, than that they had lately subdu'd.

These Sea-port Towns giving entrance to fresh and numerous Fleets of *Norwegians*, *Danes*, and *Oostmans*;* insomuch that the *Irish* were forc'd once more to have recourse to their Arms.* And here it was that *Maolseachelvin*'s Heart became mollified, and once more gave consent (when the Kingdom should be freed of its Foes) that *Murchoe* should Marry his Daughter.*

The two Lovers had now admittance to see each other, and with a bleeding Heart the Charming *Dooneflaith* made known to her dear *Murchoe* the reason why she us'd that severity to him at his return from the former Battle: *Murchoe* lov'd too well to think any of the fault was on her side, and was now the most happy Man in the World. Her Father, the King, made him his General, but the Occasion was urgent, and he was hasted away, having scarce time to take his Leave.

However, he had with a thousand soft and passionate Speeches already parted with *Dooneflaith*, and was now come to *Maolseachelvin*, who receiv'd him with all the expressions of tenderness that could be. 'Go Valiant Youth, says the King to him, go, and return Crown'd with Laurels of Victory; revenge the hard Usage you have suffer'd, on those barbarous Infidels; forgive my Rashness, and believe I now set no difference betwixt thee and my own Child. No, my dear Son, for so henceforth I will call thee, and tho' your Father shun all my Advancements, I thus will embrace his Son. Go then, Victorious *Murchoe*, Head our Men; my chearful Soldiers long to see their Chief, they think the time you lose in my embraces, an Age, in their impatience'.

'Now mighty Monarch, says *Murchoe* to him, you show'r such Blessings on my Head, give me such Courage, and such Hopes, that if I Conquer not, let me hereafter bear the Coward brand; the Power you give me, united with the thoughts of my *Dooneflaith*, shall make me Conqueror where e'er I go, and sweep your numerous Enemies from off the Earth'.

After many endearing Discourses, *Murchoe* took Horse, and went to the Army, who wellcom'd him with loud shouts of Joy; and where he found such Stout and Resolute *Irish-men*, that where-ever he came, he carried Victory on his Sword's Point; while his Father *Bryan* no less fearing the loss of the Kingdom again, in the Southern parts of the Country did such things as would almost seem incredible, and in a short time was Crown'd King of *Munster*, still Conquering where e'er he went, and soon after subdu'd one half of the Nation. Nor did he put a stop to his irresistable Force, till he was publickly Elected, and made Monarch of all *Ireland*, the Nobility and Princes deposing *Maolseachelvin*, to make way for *Bryan*, giving him leave to live, which is the greatest misery that can befall a Monarch after the loss of a Diadem.

Bryan now being King of all *Ireland*, thought himself sufficiently reveng'd for the slights which *Maolseachelvin* had put on his Son, and commanded *Murchoe* to come home to his Palace, which then he kept at *Tomond*,* to the unspeakable trouble and affliction of the two Lovers, who now were taking, as they fear'd, their last leaves of each other.

'Oh! my adorable Saint, says the afflicted *Murchoe* to *Dooneflaith*, how unfortunate have all my Undertakings been! How Cruel is my Fate; that now, when I thought my Happiness beyond the reach of any Misfortune, I find it dash'd, by that which I hop'd would have been its chief stay. Now my *Dooneflaith*, my miseries come rolling upon me, and soon will overwhelm me! Oh! insupportable Cruelty, I must leave my Love! leave her, (good Heavens defend,) I fear for ever; But witness Gods, and all you Saints above, though absent from my sight I'll ne'er forget thee; Hopes, (once to bless me with thy sight again,) shall buoy me up through all my Sea of Sorrows, if my dear Love but promise to be constant.—'

Dooneflaith could not hear him make such a scruple, without shewing how much it touch'd her Heart. 'Oh, cruel *Murchoe*! said she, do you take part against me! And if I will be constant! Barbarous doubt! have you thus long beheld me stand the shock of all Misfortunes, even when Ambition, and a Monarch's Crown, would have shook the most firm and constant of our Sex; and can you make that scruple now? If I'll be constant! Oh Heaven! that If, will stab me to the Soul! you've found the only means, next to your hating me, that could undo my peace, you almost tear my Heart up by the roots; what! doubt an Heart like mine, that is made up of nothing else but Love and Constancy! But I forgive Thee *Murchoe*, I know 'twas but the overflowings of thy tender fear, and the excess of a too powerful Passion; and to confirm my dearest *Murchoe*'s Mind, bear Witness for me now, Oh all ye Gods, and show'r upon me all your dreadful Vengeance, if what I say be not sincere and true, when in your absence I forgot my Faith, either in thought or deed; either for Threats, or all the Proffers in the World; if from this Heart *Murchoe* be ever absent, then let the Furies tear me

Limb by Limb, and Dogs and Wolves devour my scatter'd Carcass'.

'No more, says *Murchoe*, I believe my Saint, and ever shall retain these precious words in the chief Records of my memory'. They were forc'd soon after this to part; but with such languishing and dying looks, as if they ne'er should meet again: how many times did *Murchoe* go to the Door, and then return again, loath to depart, printing his soft Lips on her fair Hand, and she as often wish'd they might dwell there for ever; they sighed, and wept, then wiped their watry Cheeks, making exchange of Hearts at eithers Eyes; at last, as though both their words had been prompted by one Soul, they together cry'd, the Gods preserve, and ever be your Comfort.

Murchoe having taken his leave, went directly, but most heavily, towards his Fathers Palace in *Tomond*, call'd *Cean-Choradh*,* where he was welcom'd by *Bryan*, and the whole Court; but what were all the welcomes in the World to him, since his *Dooneflaith*'s Voice was wanting in the Consort, the Musick was not sweet or charming, he wholly bent his Thoughts on her, and Day or Night, she was the subject of his Mind; tho' he was ever accounted Devout, yet now the welfare and happiness of his afflicted Mistress, threw him on his Knees almost each hour.

His Father, and the whole Court could not but greatly wonder at this mighty Change; he grew Pale, neglected Meat, and Sleep, walk'd all the Day in melancholy places, seeking recesses, where the hunted Beasts scarce dar'd to enter, they were so dark and dismal; where, with his folded Arms across his troubled Breast, he'd vent the Griefs which rankled at his Heart.

Into one of these Places was it, that his Father one day follow'd him, and having privately listned to his usual Complaints, when the poor Prince had thrown himself down, extended on a rugged Rock, his Eyes (like Rivers which had broke their Banks) pour'd forth a flood of Tears, with Groans and Sighs, which almost rent the Vault.

'How Happy, said he to himself, had *Murchoe* been, had Heaven been pleas'd he should have perish'd in his Countries Service, his loss perhaps would then have touch'd his Fathers hardned Heart; he would have then perhaps shed one Tear, and with a sigh, have pitty'd his untimely End: But now he thinks I breath, he thinks I live; when as, alas! these signs I give of Life, are but the Tokens of uneasie Death; for I am Dead to all the World, insensible of every thing, but Love; and tho' I move, and sometimes walk about, 'tis but my more substantial Ghost.—'

He was going on, when *Bryan* interrupted him: 'What *Murchoe*, said he, is the Cause that thus thou spendest thy Youthful time in Cells? Thus pine, and like a Woman drown thy self in Tears? Thus leave the mighty Business of the World, and bend thy Thoughts on a fantastick Trifle? Thus shun thy Friends, and seek these solitary Shades? Rouze up, for shame, awake thee from these Idle Dreams; thy Father bids thee, and a King Commands, thy bleeding Country wants thy aid: Ambition should methinks inflame thy Heart, and banish Love from that too noble Seat. Make thy self worthy to be my Successor; what? can the sprightly *Murchoe* lie dissolving in Tears, when all the Land is almost drown'd in Blood? Think on a Crown, think of a Monarch's Power, and see how poorly Love will shew to these; or were those out of reach, and that thy Hopes stood not so fair as now they do, think on thy Honour, and thy future Fame'.

'O sacred Sir, replies the Prince, can you behold these ruines of your Son? Look on, and see him sink in sorrow, and not extend a Parent's Hand to help him? O Sir, remember you your self was young, Lov'd and Ador'd, and knew no happiness but in my Mothers sight: I do but tread your steps, walk in that Path which all the World goes once; say but *Dooneflaith* shall be mine, and you will raise me unto Life again; without Her, Honour, Titles, Power, nay even a Crown it self, have nothing Charming in them'.

Bryan could no longer hear him sue in vain; but told him, if he would take Arms, and shew himself once more in the Field, and, according to his wonted Custom, come home laden with Victory, he would so much indulge his Love, that, if after this, he still continued in that Humour, he'd use his utmost Power to make him Happy.

The Prince overjoy'd with this Promise, went home with his Father, and in a few days after, Headed a brave Army against his Country's Enemies; Victory still follow'd wheresoe'er he fought, and his Courage and Conduct were not a small cause of the Renown and Glory that accru'd to his Father: For 'tis Remarkable, that *Bryan Boraimh* defeated the *Danes* and their Confederates in Twenty five bloody pitch'd Battles;* he was accounted one of the most Puissant and Noble Monarchs of the *Milesian* Race; and tho' he liv'd not to see these Invaders quite expell'd the Kingdom, yet he fought in the last Battle, that gave them their Overthrow; having in his Life time reduc'd the Kingdom (especially towards the latter end of his Reign) to so tranquil and quiet a State, that *Ireland* was become all peaceable and flourishing. Nor were there to be seen any *Danes*, but such who liv'd quietly under his Government, and were either Merchants, Handycrafts-men, or Artificers, who had their chief Residence in *Dublin*, *Weixford*, *Waterford*, *Cork*, or *Limerick*;* and tho' they were a considerable Number of them, yet not so many, nor so Potent, but that he thought should they at any time Rebell, he could Master them at his Pleasure.

Murchoe seeing no Comfort accrue to him in all this general Joy, for he alone was excluded the benefit of Tranquility the whole Nation pertook, the Conquests and Honour he won, added more Trouble to his Soul, since he could not yet obtain his Father's Consent, he avoided as much as he could the Pleasures of the Court, and betook himself wholly to the Country, where, in unspeakable Torments, he wasted his time in Complaints. But being one day near the House of *Maolmordh Mac Murchoe** his Uncle, whose Sister by name *Garmlaigh*,* Bryan his Father had Marry'd, he thought to pass some time in a Visit to him, and was very kindly receiv'd.

But *Bryan* having an occasion for Timber for the finishing some Ships he had begun, especially some Masts, he sent to his Brother-in-law *Maolmordh* to furnish him with them, to which he consented, partly out of fear to deny him, and partly for Kindred sake, he went himself to see them cut down, and assisted with his Men, those who were sent for them, in the getting them over a Mountain; to which they say (some difference happening amongst the People) he put his Hand to himself, and in the action broke off the Gold Clasps that fastned a rich fring'd Mantle of Silk which *Bryan* had sent him. At length, he with his Nephew *Murchoe*, came to *Cean-Choradh*.

But no sooner did he arrive at *Tomond*, and had gone to his Sister *Garmlaigh*'s Apartment to give her a Visit, and acquainted her how he came to break off his Clasps, which he desir'd her to get mended again for him; but in a rage she threw the whole Mantle into the fire and burnt it, reproaching him with meanness of Spirit, in so unworthily subjecting himself, and his People of *Linster*,* whereof he was King, to *Bryan*, altho' he was her own Husband.

'How basely, said she, becomes it the Blood which thou sharest with me, to fear the displeasure of any, much less one who has made himself my equal by taking me to his Wife? How much below the Honour and Dignity of the King of

Linster is it, thus like a Bondsman or Slave, to lend thy assistance, and like a Coward, grant whatever he demands from thee'.

These words, (tho' at present he made her no reply) sunk deep in his Heart, so taking his leave of her, he went into the Presence, where he found a Nobleman and *Murchoe* playing a Game at Chess,* (*Maolmordh* being touch'd to the quick with the Reproof that his Sister had given him, and no longer able to stifle the sense he had of his Fault) advis'd him who was playing with *Murchoe* on some Draught, which lost his Nephew the Game.

Murchoe, who had not been us'd to receive such Indignities, (for it was done in so palpable a manner, as he could take it for no less) being highly displeas'd, told his Uncle *Maolmordh* King of *Linster*, in a deriding manner, 'That if the Advice he had formerly given to the Rebel *Danes* been no worse, they had not so easily lost the Battle at *Gleaun Mama*;* yet notwithstanding his mighty Policy, he could not win them the Field'.

Maolmordh, being stung with this jear,* in a fury reply'd, 'However my Advice succeeded at that time, the next that perhaps I shall give to the *Danes*, shall prove better to your Cost'. So in a discontented Humour was departing; when the Prince *Murchoe* told him; 'It should never break one moment of his Rest to countermine what ever Projects he could design; and withal told him he defy'd him'.

Whereupon the King of *Linster* retir'd to his Chamber, and would not (although he was sent for by *Bryan*) come down to his Supper; but flinging himself on his Bed, pass'd all that Night in the extreamest anxiety of Spirit, that could be imagin'd; and early the next Morning, before any of the Court were stirring, takes Horse, and posts away for *Linster*, where his Heart was so full (what with the rebukes his Sister had made him, and the defiance his Nephew had given him) that he had no way to ease it, but by giving, if he could, a stint to their Insolence, by making them to know, that they had rouz'd a sleeping Lyon,* whose Fury and Rage should not be allay'd by any thing but their utter destruction.

The next day he assembles the Chief of his Nobles, and the Gentry, and represents to them the Indignity that had been put upon them in the Person of their King; and so aggravates the Matter, that he drew them all to his side, and made them all on fire to revenge it; by throwing off their Allegiance and Fidelity to *Bryan*, and joyning their Power to that of the *Danes*, and in return to the Challenge that *Murchoe* had made him, to send him another.

Having gain'd his Designs at Home, he flies with all speed to *Dublin*, and there engages the chief of the *Danes*,* to send away instantly to their Master, the King of *Denmark*,* for a strong and powerful Supply to pull down the Grandeur and haughty Pride of *Bryan*, and to destroy their, and his most mortal Enemies; which on the word of a King, he promis'd to perform, would they be assistant.

While Messengers were sent over into *Denmark*, he returns Home again; where (with all the hast* he could use, and most indefatigable pains) he prepares for a War; nor was it long e'er he goes to *Dublin* again; where, at his arrival, two of the King of *Denmark*'s Sons (*Carolus Knutus*, and *Andreas* his Brother)* Landed, at the Head of twelve thousand *Danes*,* which they had brought along with them, whom (after he had kindly receiv'd, and refresh'd them well) he forthwith, knowing delays in such Cases would be dangerous, and give his Enemies too much time to Unite) by an Herald sends *Bryan* a bold Defiance, daring him to meet him in a spacious Field at *Clantarf*,* within two Miles of *Dublin*.

Bryan had no sooner receiv'd this Challenge; but (making what speed he was able) joyn'd together all the Forces of *Munster*, *Connaught*, and *Meath*, for those of *Ulster*, he sent not to them, being unwilling to stay till they should come up; and believing he had Power enough out of those other three Provinces to encounter the Enemy.

The Prince *Murchoe* his Son was sent to those in *Meath*, where he once more got a sight of his charming *Dooneflaith*, and whom (after the success of the Battle) he had a Promise from *Bryan* his Father, that he should Marry.

Never did two faithful Lovers meet with such Joy, and *Dooneflaith* even blest the Causers of this War, which had made her so happy with the presence of her dear *Murchoe*. *Maolseachelvin*, tho' depos'd from the Monarchy, had great Interest in the Province of *Meath*, and soon rais'd such Forces, as perchance none else could have done; which *Bryan* understanding, made him General of that part of the Army, and sent for his Son back to himself.

But if the Meeting of this Amorous Pair was so full of Joy and Content, yet their Parting was such as is not to be express'd; they took their leaves of each other, with such unwillingness, and regret, that their Separation seem'd to have rent their Hearts asunder.

Murchoe was not altogether so overwhelm'd as he had formerly been, since his Hopes now stood fair, in a few days, to Crown all his Sufferings with the enjoyment of his Charming *Dooneflaith*: But the disconsolate Fair-One, felt such Pangs, at his taking his leave, as gave those who stood by (especially her Father) cause to suspect they were but too fatal Omens. And he being willing they should have all the liberty the little time he had to see her, to say what they pleas'd privately together, he withdrew, and left them to themselves.

Now it was that *Dooneflaith* vented the tenders of her Soul in such a manner, that *Murchoe* himself could hardly stay with her, to hear the Complaints which she made of her hard Destiny. 'Oh *Murchoe*, said she, you are going to leave me for ever; I have something here at my Heart, that prompts my Soul to think *Murchoe* will never return to his *Dooneflaith* again, my presaging Heart fore-bodes, that the Victory which you are going to win, will be cause of Joy to all *Ireland*, but my unfortunate self'.

Murchoe us'd all Arguments that could be thought of, to dissipate her Fears; And told her, that his Courage, guarded by the hopes of her Love, would make him do things that should fill the Trumpet of Fame to the end of the World. 'I go, my Charming *Dooneflaith*, says he, to set this Kingdom in Peace, that so I with the more freedom may quietly enjoy the Blessing the Gods would bestow at the end of the Conquest; and that *Ireland* might be so settled, that he no more might have cause to quit her soft Arms to follow the Wars'.

'Go *Murchoe*, (reply'd she, with such languishing looks, and so dying a tone as almost made him alter his firm Resolution;) Go and fight for thy Country, Go and Conquer, Go and—(I would fain say) return again to my Arms: But—Oh! something here at my Heart will not let me believe the Heavens will make me so Happy. No, my *Murchoe*, these Eyes will never behold thee again; and the next Embrace thou hast, will be that cold one of Death. Methinks I see my dearest *Murchoe*, all pale and cold, stuck through with a thousand Darts and Arrows; his breathless Corps spurting fresh streams of Blood; when I, unhappy I, come by, who am his Murderer'.

'No more my Charmer, says *Murchoe* to her, drive these idle Thoughts away, they are but Dreams which will disturb thy Rest; I shall return, I know it by my Heart; (Oh! that I did, said he to himself,) Or say I dy'd, I paid but Nature's Debt, what you and I, and all must do at last; my Fall shall not be mean, and thousands braver Men shall bear me Company. Oh! *Dooneflaith*, what Comfort will it be, how will it soften Death, and blunt its sharpest Dart, to think I die belov'd by thee!'

While they were Embracing, in order to Part, *Maolseachelvin* came in, and told him he must make all hast possible with his Forces, for all the others which they expected were come in but his.

The Prince, as eager as he was to meet his proud Challenger, and not think of leaving his Mistress behind; wherefore, by her Consent, and joint intreaty, *Maolseachelvin* promis'd to bring her with him; this at last something appeas'd the Sorrow of both; and *Murchoe*, after a thousand soft Kisses, and Embraces, and as many Sighs, and Tears on both sides, took Horse, and posted before to his Father, and the next day after *Maolseachelvin* follow'd with his Army; and at the Rear of that, the beautiful *Dooneflaith*.

In a few days after, the Armies of the three Provinces joyn'd all together, and march'd in good order to the Place appointed, being a spacious Field near *Clantarfe*,* call'd *Magnealta*,* where they beheld *Maolmordh* at the Head of a vast Army; being sixteen Thousand *Danes*, together with all the Forces he could raise in *Leinster*, which was divided into three Battalions; that of the Right Wing Commanded by *Carolus Knutus*, that on the Left by his Brother *Andreas*, (the two Sons of the *Danish* King) and the Main Body *Maolmordh* took care of himself.

Bryan drew up his Army much after the same Order, committing the Right Wing thereof to *Maolseachelvin*, the Left he Commanded himself; and (at the intreaty of his Son *Murchoe*, that he might oppose *Maolmordh* himself, who had given him a Challenge) the main Body was under his Conduct.

Early next Morning (it being *Good Friday*)* both Armies drew near, and after a short time the fatal Signal was given on both sides, never did two Armies encounter more fiercely; the shouts and cries, with the Thundering noise of the Drums and, sound of Trumpets, were enough to rend the very Roof of Heaven. Nor for half the Day could it be decided upon which side hovering Victory would light; and had *Maolseachelvin* (who Headed the Army of *Meath*) came up, they had soon turn'd the Scale. But he, remembring the Affront of *Bryan*, who made him be Depos'd, to make way for himself, as soon as the Signal was given, stood off with his Men, and was only a Spectator of the most bloody and terrible Fight that ever was Acted on the Tragick Theatre of *Irish* Ground. Nay, tho' at one time he saw his own Country-men begin to give way, and the *Danes* in a probability of winning the Day, yet did he stand unmov'd.

Bryan who Headed the Left Wing of the Army, being Old (for he was now above fourscore and eight)* having to do with *Carolus*, who was both Valiant and Young, was in the Battle struck from his Horse, and had not Prince *Murchoe* come timely to his Rescue, he had been trod to pieces by the Enemy; which nevertheless so bruis'd and wounded him, that he was forc'd to be carry'd to his Tent, leaving the Charge of his Army to Prince *Murchoe*.

Now was the time that he had the whole Fate of *Ireland* depending upon his Sword, he did such wondrous Actions as surpass'd all belief, and so bravely behav'd himself, as tho' he had been some God sent down from above. He (spight of all their Forces, thinking of the Liberty of his Country, and Love of his dear *Dooneflaith*) made such breaches in their Main Body, that notwithstanding they had all the Inspiration of Courage, that Martial-Conduct, Ambition, Glory, Revenge, and Despair could afford them, yet so great was *Murchoe*'s Courage, and Conduct so happy, that the *Danish* and *Leinster* Forces could no longer withstand him; having with his own Hand first slain *Maolmordh*, who was the first occasion of this War; and then at two several times the two Sons of the King of *Denmark*; whose Loss so disheartned the Enemy, that they gave way, to an easie, though dear-bought Victory; for *Murchoe* being too far engag'd among the *Danish* Horse, tho' over-power'd with Number, fought 'till he had made a Rampart of dead Bodies about him, which for some time secur'd him from Fate; but an unlucky accidental Arrow laid him dead upon a Pyramid of his fallen Enemies.

Yet for all this, did not the resolute *Irish* loose one foot of Ground, or one bit of their Courage; but rather, spur'd on by Revenge, made the *Danes* pay dear for his Loss, and in a short time became sole Masters of the Field. Thus without the assistance of *Maolseachelvin*, were the *Danes* overcome; one whereof, whose Name was *Bruador*,* being Commander of a *Danish* Party, and who with his Men flying in the General Rout, was forc'd to take that way where *Bryan* the Monarch's Pavilion was pitch'd; into which (as he was passing by) he entred; and seeing the King, whom he had formerly known, *Bryan* suspecting no such thing, having totally gain'd the Battle, basely Murder'd him as he lay wounded in his Bed: But he soon had the Reward due to so Treacherous an Act; for he, and all who follow'd him, were by his Guards, and the Pursuers, cut all to pieces.

Maolseachelvin after this, put in for his Share, and made himself once more Monarch of *Ireland*. Tho' his Daughter no sooner heard the Death of her Lover, but as though she had lain down to Sleep, flung her self on her Bed, and without so much as one Groan, Sigh, or Murmur, she cry'd, *My* Murchoe *calls me, and I must go to him*; so dy'd in the presence of her Father, and the rest of the Nobility, who had escap'd in the Battle, for there were but few left alive: and on the Monarch's Side, besides Bryan himself, and the Renowned Prince *Murchoe* his Son, were kill'd in this Battle, Seven petty

Kings,* most of the Princes and Nobility of *Munster* and *Conaught*, and four Thousand of meaner Degree.

But on the other side, *viz*. that of the *Danes* and *Leinster* Party, were Slain *Maolmordh Mac-Murchoe*, the King of *Leinster*, who was the Original Cause of this Slaughter, with all his Principal Nobles, and three Thousand Common Soldiers; together with *Knutus*, and *Andreas*, the two Sons of the King of Denmark, and all their Great Commanders, with six Thousand seven Hundred of the New-come Forces from *Denmark*, that they had brought over with them, and four Thousand of the old *Danes*, who were, before their coming, in *Ireland*. In all the Slaughter on both Sides, that Day, amounted to seven Thousand seven Hundred Men, besides Kings, Princes, Commanders, and other Noble-Men.

Some time after this Battle, *Maolseachelvin*, (who now the second time sat on the Monarchical Throne of *Ireland*,* and was the last Monarch of the *Milesian* Race) took *Dublin*, Sack'd it, Burnt it, and Slew in it all those *Danes* who had made their escape thither from the Battle of *Clantarfe*.

The next Year, in the said *Maolseachelvin*'s Reign, *Huaghaire Mac-Duniling Mac-Tuatil*,* another King of *Leinster*, who succeeded *Maolmordh*, tho' of a more Noble Race, and better Interested for the Good of his Country, gave a mighty overthrow, (which was the last that was given) to *Stetirick* the Son of *Aomlaibh*,* and the *Danes* of *Dublin*, who after the Battle of *Clantarfe*, and the Burning of Dublin by *Maolseachelvin*, had once more Recruited from the *Isle of Man*, and other Islands, which were yet in Possession of the *Danes*, but were now totally destroy'd throughout all *Ireland*.

Thus did that Warlike and Ancient Kingdom free it self from the Tyranny of its mortal Enemy the *Danes*.

FINIS.

BOOKS lately Publish'd.

EXILIUS: Or, The Banish'd *Roman*. A New entertaining ROMANCE. Written (after the manner of *Telemachus*) for the Instruction of some young Ladies of Quality. By Mrs. *Jane Barker*. containing the following Histories, *viz*.

- I. *Clelia* and *Marcellus*: Or, The Constant Lovers.
- II. The Reward of Vertue: Or, The Adventures of *Clarinthia* and *Lysander*.
- III. The Lucky Escape: Or, The Fate of *Ismenus*.
- IV. *Clodius* and *Scipiana*: Or, The Beautiful Captive.
- V. *Piso*: Or, The Lewd Courtier.
- VI. The Happy Recluse: Or, The Charms of Liberty.
- VII. The Transformation: Or, The Amours of *Cordiala*.
- VIII. The Fair Widow: Or, False Friend.

To which is added, The Scene of Pleasure; being the Description of a Compleat Garden. Price 3*s*.

The *Sincere VIRGIN*: Or, The Amours of *Bosvil* and *Galesia*. A NOVEL. By Mrs. *Barker*. Price 1*s*. Stitch'd, 1*s*. 6*d*. Bound.

HANOVER *Tales*: Or, The History of Count *Fradonia* and the Unfortunate *Baritia*. Done out of *French*. Price 1*s*. 6*d*. Stitch'd, 2*s*. Bound.

POEMS upon Several Occasions. By the late Reverend Mr. *POMFRET*, Author of the *Choice*. Price 2*s*.

The Adventures of RIVELLA: Or, The History of the Author of the *Atalantis*; with Secret *Memoirs* and *Manners* of several Considerable *Persons* Her Cotemporaries. With a Compleat Key. Price 2*s*. 6*d*.

The PETTICOAT: An Heroi-Comical Poem in Two Books. By Mr. GAY, Jun. Price 1*s*.

Printed for *E. Curll* at the *Dial* and *Bible*, and *J. Hooke* at the *Flower-de-Luce*, both against St. *Dunstan*'s Church in *Fleetstreet*. Where Gentlemen and Ladies may be Furnish'd with all the New Books, Plays, and Pamphlets that come out.

Notes

p. 33 *Irish Tales*: Works of fiction whose titles draw attention to their Irish subject-matter or characters are extremely uncommon in the late-seventeenth and early-eighteenth centuries and, where they occur, mostly derogatory, as with *The Wild-Irish Captain, or Villany display'd truly and faithfully related* (London, 1692), or *The Irish Rogue; or, the comical history of the life and actions of Teague O'Divelley, from his birth to the present year, 1690* (London [1690]). The anonymous *Vertue Rewarded; or, the Irish Princess* (London, 1693) is a rare exception.

p. 33 *'Instructive Histories'*: The Horatian ideal of literature as being 'dulce et utile' or 'pleasing and useful [or "instructive"]' was commonplace in the eighteenth century. *Irish Tales*, however, is the first work of fiction to declare itself an 'instructive' history, though it would shortly be followed by a new edition of John Lyly's popular *Euphues* (1579), which appeared under the title *The False Friend and Inconstant Mistress: An Instructive Novel* (1718), and Jane Barker's *A patch-work screen for the ladies; or, love and virtue recommended: in a collection of instructive novels* (1723).

p. 33 *Mrs. Sarah Butler*: For the author of *Irish Tales*, see 'Introduction', pp. 12–14.

p. 33 *E. Curll and J. Hooke*: Edmund Curll (d. 1747) was a prolific and notorious London bookseller who started in business around 1706. Known as publisher of a wide range of miscellaneous works he unscrupulously produced unauthorized versions of works by Jonathan Swift and Alexander Pope, among others. In 1716, Curll published similarly unauthorized versions of poems by Pope, Gay, and Lady Mary Wortley Montagu in *Court Poems*, provoking Pope to take his revenge in two pamphlets beginning with *A full and true account of a horrid and barbarous revenge by poison, on the body of Mr. Edmund Curll, bookseller; with a faithful copy of his last will and testament* (1716). John Hooke was active in London between 1714 and 1730.

p. 35 *The Epistle Dedicatory*: The dedication was written by the miscellaneous writer Charles Gildon (*c.*1665–1724). In his epistle, Gildon refers to the sheets of *Irish Tales* 'falling into my Hands', though how they might have done so is an unanswerable, if intriguing, question. Born into an English Roman Catholic family, Gildon was originally intended for the priesthood; subsequently, he professed deism before conforming to the Church of England around 1700. In the early 1690s, Gildon was in contact with the bookseller, John Dunton (1659–1732), who later spent time in Ireland, writing several works about his experiences there. A Whig in politics, Gildon shared the earl of Lincoln's political allegiances but had no obvious reason for dedicating *Irish Tales* to him.

p. 35 *Earl of Lincoln*: Henry Clinton, seventh earl of Lincoln (1684–1728). Given the Jacobite sympathies evident in *Irish Tales*, this Hanoverian politician, who had been Paymaster-General during the Jacobite rebellion of 1715, is an exceptionally odd choice for the dedication by Gildon. For the Jacobitism of the novel, see 'Introduction', pp 12–13, 22.

p. 35 *Fair Authress*: For the identity of the author of *Irish Tales*, see 'Introduction', pp 12–14.

p. 35 *HEROIC LOVE and all the PATRIOT VIRTUES*: Heroic love, understood as the idealized love of kings, queens, princes and princesses, described in the context of a personal struggle between the competing demands of public duty and private desire, is clearly in evidence in *Irish Tales*. In 1700, John Dryden had written:

> A Patriot, both the King and Country serves;
> Prerogative and Privilege preserves:
> Of Each, our Laws the certain Limit show;
> One must not ebb, nor t'other overflow
>
> ('To my Honour'd Kinsman, John Driden', *Fables Ancient and Modern* [1700], ll. 171–4)

which is perhaps close to Gildon's notion of active devotion to king and country. If so, it emphasizes Gildon's limited understanding of the fact that, for *Irish Tales*, the *patria* is the island of Ireland which, in both its ancient and modern states, is characterized by its resistance to foreign invasion, Norse or English.

p. 35 *in the most dubious and difficult of Times*: The Jacobite Rebellion of 1715 was intended to place on the throne James Francis Edward Stuart (1688–1766), son of the deposed James II (1633–1701), known to his supporters as James III of England and Ireland and James VIII of Scotland, and to his opponents as the 'Old Pretender'. Beginning in August 1715, the Rebellion had been effectively defeated in both Scotland and England by November of that year, the Old Pretender landing in Scotland belatedly in December 1715 from France, to which he returned on 4 February 1716. Though the expected rebellion in Ireland never took place and the British rebellion was a failure, the events of 1715 nevertheless shook the Hanoverian dynasty that had begun the previous year with the accession to the throne of the Elector of Hanover as George I.

p. 35 *all true BRITONS*: Great Britain had become a political reality following the 1707 Act of Union between England and Scotland.

p. 35 *best of Kings*: George I (1660–1727), who acceded to the thrones of Great Britain and Ireland, in 1714, following the death of Queen Anne.

p. 36 [*those*] ... *who had then the Publick Management of Affairs*: Gildon alludes to the Tories in the last years of Queen Anne's reign. The strong party feeling characteristic of the period between 1710 and 1714 came to a head over the terms of the Treaty of Utrecht (1713) designed to bring an end to the War of the Spanish Succession. The accession of George I resulted in a Whig administration that sought to settle old scores with its political opponents, so that leading Tory politicians and writers, including Robert Harley, first earl of Oxford, and Matthew Prior, were imprisoned on charges of treason. Two other leading Tory writers, Jonathan Swift and Alexander Pope, also fell into official disfavour and Gildon quarrelled with both over literary and political differences.

p. 36 *ARTS as well as Arms*: That military and literary glory were complementary was a commonplace in the early-eighteenth century; cf, Pope's lines:

> *Learning* and *Rome* alike in Empire grew,
> And *Arts* still *follow'd* where her *Eagles flew*
> (Alexander Pope, *Essay on Criticism* [1711], ll. 683–4)

p. 36 MILTIADES: Miltiades (*c.*540–489 BC), an Athenian military commander who led his men to victory over the Persian army at the Battle of Marathon (490).

p. 36 *VIRGIL, HORACE, VARIUS, TUCCA*: Virgil (70–19 BC), Roman poet, celebrated as author of the *Aeneid*; Horace (65–8 BC), Roman lyric poet, satirist and literary critic; Varius Rufus (1st century BC), Roman poet and friend of Virgil and Horace; Plotius Tucca (1st century BC), friend of Virgil who, with Varius Rufus, edited the *Aeneid* after the poet's death; all were associated with the so-called 'Augustan age' of Roman literature.

p. 36 *ablest Statesman, and most illustrious Emperor*: Gaius Octavius Caesar, the emperor Augustus (63 BC– AD 14), whose reign was often considered to be the high point of Latin literature.

p. 37 *a Nobleman ... Three Hundred Guineas*: Charles Gildon had previously rehearsed a fuller version of this story concerning the difficulty of finding a generous and noble patron: 'One of these Great Men not many Years ago, gave 300 Guineas to a *French* Piper for a few Tunes on the *Haut Bois*, and afterwards gave a Man of no Mean Figure in the Common-wealth of Letters, but 50 for the Dedication of a very valuable *Folio*', *Les Soupirs de la Grand Britaigne: or, The Groans of Great Britain* (London, 1713), p. 32.

p. 37 *SIDNEYS and SACKVILES*: Sir Philip Sidney (1554–86), English poet, soldier, and courtier, author of *Arcadia,* the sonnet sequence *Astrophel and Stella*, and *A Defence of Poetry*; Thomas Sackville, first earl of Dorset (1536–1608), poet, lord high treasurer, and chancellor of Oxford University.

p. 37 *Poetry ... natural Growth of the Clime*: The connection between climate and the natural genius of a nation was something of a commonplace in the eighteenth century; Dryden had touched on the notion in his *Essay of Dramatick Poesie* (1668) and the idea had been explored more recently by Joseph

Addison in *The Spectator* (1711–12), esp. numbers 83, 162 and 371.

p. 37 *all* POETRY *is an* IMITATION: The observation occurs in *Poetics*, I, I, by Aristotle (384–322 BC). The idea that all fables are imitations of actions is central to the *Poetics* and the comparison between dramatic (especially tragic) and epic poetry is to be found, for instance, in *Poetics*, I, V.

p. 37 *Milesian Tales*: Gildon's reference is to the group of works written by the Greek author Aristides of Miletus (2nd century BC), all but fragments of which are lost; the name came to be associated with any fictions recounting tales of love and adventure. Confusingly, contemporary Irish writers referred to the original inhabitants of Ireland as 'Milesians' (see n. to 'The Preface', p. 39, 'the Milesian race' below). Edmund Curll published a subsequent edition of Sarah Butler's book under the title *Milesian Tales* (London, 1719), but it is doubtful that a play on the two different meanings of 'Milesian' was apparent to many contemporary novel readers.

p. 37 HELIODORUS: Heliodorus of Emesa (3rd–4th century AD) was the author of a Greek novel, the *Aethiopica or Theagenes and Charicleia*; the work was rendered into English as *The Triumphs of Love and Constancy: A Romance containing the Heroick Amours of Theagenes & Chariclea* (1687), the last five books being the work of the Irish-born Nahum Tate (*c.*1652–1715).

p. 37 *Tast*: i.e. taste.

p. 37 *Books of* TALES: Despite Gildon's reference to 'so many Books of TALES', comparatively few volumes of prose 'tales' had been published in the thirty or so years prior to the publication of *Irish Tales*. Most of these, moreover, were translations, including a rendering of the *Decameron* as *The Novels and Tales of the renowned John Boccaccio* (5th ed. 1684); Thomas d'Urfey, *Tales tragical and comical* (1704), which mixed prose and verse tales taken from the Italian, French and Spanish; *The Persian and the Turkish Tales, Compleat* (London, 1714); Ambrose Philips's translation, *The Thousand and One Days: Persian Tales*, 3 vols (London, 1714–5); and Thomas-Simon Gueullette, *A Thousand and One Quarters of Hours; being Tartarian Tales* (1716). Clearly intended for the moment, shortly after the accession of the Elector of Hanover as George I, was the reissue as *Hanover Tales* of another translation from the French, the *German Atalantis* (1715). Many of these were designed for male and female readers alike but the anonymous *The Ladies Tales: exemplified in the vertues and vices of the quality, with reflections* (London, 1714), with its strong defence of female learning, was principally aimed at women readers. So were Marie-Catherine (Madame) d'Aulnoy's *The History of the Tales of the Fairies* (1716), whose title-page affirms it to be 'Dedicated to the *LADIES* of Great-Britain', and Jane Barker's *Exilius; or, The Banish'd Roman: A New entertaining ROMANCE, written ... for the Instruction of some young Ladies of Quality* (1715), advertised by Curll as containing eight numbered and named 'Histories' (though the advertisement is not reflected on the title-page itself). In describing itself as a volume of 'tales', while being a through-composed narrative,

Irish Tales is highly unusual, and perhaps unique, for its time.

p. 38 *their Foundation is laid on true History*: For the connection between history and early fiction, see 'Introduction', p. 18.

p. 39 *the Milesian Race*: Seventeenth- and eighteenth-century historians and antiquarians referred to the origins of the inhabitants of Ireland as 'Milesians', the name deriving from Milesius (Míl Espáine), a fabulous Spanish king, whose sons supposedly invaded Ireland around 1300 BC. The story derives from the early-medieval pseudo-history, *Lebor Gabála*, or *Book of Invasions*, and is to be found in *Foras Feasa ar Éirinn* (written *c.*1634), by Seathrún Céitinn (*c.*1580–*c.*1644), known in English as Geoffrey (or Jeoffrey) Keating, and in Roderick O'Flaherty's Latin history of Ireland, *Ogygia* (1685), among other works cited by Sarah Butler. Butler here uses the term 'Milesian' in this sense while Charles Gildon used 'Milesian tales' in relation to the Greek fictions.

p. 39 *Novel*: In 1716, 'novel' had not yet acquired its modern connotations. 'Novel', 'romance', 'history' and other terms were often used interchangeably or subsumed, well into the mid-eighteenth century, under the more general term 'the new species of writing'. Attempts were made to distinguish between novels and romances – famously, for instance, by William Congreve in the preface to his *Incognita* (1692) – but these were not universally accepted. Like many contemporary fictions, *Irish Tales* combines aspects of novelist and romance discourse, in its use of historical source material combined with its 'elevated' characters (kings, princes, princesses) and its central theme of the competing themes of duty versus love, of the public versus the private (see also 'Introduction', pp 23–5 above).

p. 39 *Murchoe and Dooneflaith … Story*: As noted in the 'Introduction' (pp 17–18), *Irish Tales* draws heavily for its historical material on *Foras Feasa ar Éirinn* by Seathrún Céitinn which in 1716 circulated in Irish- and English-language manuscripts only. The first publication of *Foras Feasa* was an English-language translation by Dermod O'Connor, which appeared in London, seven years after the publication of *Irish Tales*, as *The General History of Ireland … collected by the learned Jeoffry Keating, D.D., faithfully translated from the original Irish Language, with many curious Amendments taken from the Psalter of Tara and Cashel, and other authentick Records, by Dermo'd* [sic] *O Connor, Antiquary of the Kingdom of Ireland* (London, 1723). For the spelling 'Murchoe', Butler seems to follow Peter Walsh, in his *A Prospect of the State of Ireland*; see n. to p. 40, 'Walsh … Ireland' below; in O'Connor's translation, the son of Brian is called 'Murrough', though modern historians use 'Murchad' (see also 'Appendix 1: List of names').

Sarah Butler's lengthy justification of her use of the name 'Dooneflaith' (see also n. to p. 44, 'Dooneflaith' below, and 'Appendix 1: List of names'), is necessarily confusing to readers attempting to follow the historical narrative of *Irish Tales*. Indicating that she has called her character Dooneflaith since that was the name of her mother, Butler both misremembers her source material in Keating's *General History* and glosses over her radical adaptation of two separate episodes within it. As explained in 'Appendix 1: List of names', Butler conflates two different monarchs living over a century apart: Máel Sechnaill I and Máel Sechnaill II, for the purposes of creating a powerful narrative of Irish resistance to foreign invasion. 'Dunflath' – as O'Connor renders the name in his translation of Keating – is in fact the mother, not the wife, of Máel Sechnaill II; see *General History of Ireland*, II, p. 486. Though the story of the daughter of Máel Sechnaill I and her role in the downfall of the Viking leader Turgesius (see n. to p. 41, 'Turgesius', below, and 'Appendix 1: List of Names') was widely told by writers from Gerald of Wales onwards, the only historian to name her, apparently, is the abbé James MacGeoghegan, who calls her Melcha, 'qui étoit jeune & de figure à plaire', *Histoire de l'Irlande: Ancienne et Moderne*, 3 vols (Paris, 1758–63), I, p. 384. The 'Story' of which historians 'take notice' is, in other words, a composite of two different episodes from Irish history, variously treated by different chroniclers.

p. 39 *Maolseachelvin*'s *Daughter*: For 'Maolseachelvin' or Máel Sechnaill, see preceding note and 'Appendix 1: List of names'.

p. 39 *Dr. Ketrius*: i.e. Dr. Keating. Possibly an attempt to Latinize the name of Seathrún Céitinn but the spelling of Irish names was a major headache generally for English printers in the eighteenth century and Keating's name is given as 'Keting' at its next occurrence.

p. 39 *Ireland ...one of the Principal Nations in Europe ... The Island of Saints*: The positive account of Ireland anticipated here is central to *Irish Tales*. From at least the time of Gerald of Wales, or Giraldus Cambrensis (*c.*1146–1220x23), author of *Topographia Hibernica* (*The Topography of Ireland*), accounts of Ireland by writers from the neighbouring island were generally negative and often exceptionally hostile. Sarah Butler recalls that Ireland had indeed been an important centre of learning during the Middle Ages. Irish monasteries attracted students from England and continental Europe and Irish monks, notably, St Columbanus (d. 615), travelled to found monasteries as far away as Iona in Scotland, Lindisfarne in the north of England, Annegray, Luxeuil, and Fontaines in France, St Gall in Switzerland, and Bobbio in northern Italy. The description of Ireland as 'The Island of Saints' is also used by Peter Walsh, in his *A Prospect of the State of Ireland* (1682), from which Butler quotes liberally in the following paragraphs; for Walsh see n. to p. 40, 'Walsh ... Ireland' below.

p. 40 **Bede and* †*Camden*: St Bede (673/4–735), monk and author of *The Ecclesiastical History of the English People* (731), cited in Butler's note, which contains much information about English and other European scholars who studied in Ireland and about Irish clergy, including St Aidan (Áedán), who helped convert the English; William Camden (1551–1623), historian, whose Latin *Britannia*, mentioned in Butler's note, was first published in 1586, with later, enlarged editions in 1587, 1590, 1594, and 1600. Despite the scholarly apparatus, Butler in fact took both her references verbatim from Walsh's *Prospect*, p. 56 n. (a); for Walsh see following note.

p. 40 *Walsh ... Prospect of Ireland*: Peter Walsh (*c.*1618–88), Irish Roman Catholic priest and historian, author of *A Prospect of the State of Ireland from the year of the world 1756, to the year of Christ 1652* (London, 1682). In his 'Preface to the Reader', Walsh notes that he has borrowed occasionally from writers such as Gerald of Wales, Campion, Hanmer and Spenser (see nn. to p. 40, 'Spenser ...' and 40, 'Bede ...') but continues 'when I was a young man I had read *Geoffrey Keting*'s Irish Manuscript History of *Ireland*. And now when my Lord of *Castle-Haven* would needs engage me to write something ... I remembred how about four of five year since, the *R.H.* Earl of *Anglesey*, Lord *Privy Seal*, had been pleas'd to shew me another Manuscript, being an *English* Translation of that *Irish* History of Ketings' ([np]); later in the preface, Walsh discusses the problem of rendering Irish names in non-Irish script, drawing attention also to the fact that 'my Copy of *Keting* [was] very bad in many places' (*Prospect*, 'Preface' [np.])

p. 40 *He is gone to Ireland to be bred ... mirabile claros*: Butler quotes Peter Walsh: 'in those dayes the *Saxons* flowed over into *Ireland* as to the Mart of good Literature. And that, when any was wanting here from home, it came to be a Proverb, *He is gone to* Ireland *to be bred*. Pursuant hereunto is that Distich in the life of *Sulgenus* (who flourish'd about 700 years since)

Exemplo patrum commotus amore legendi,
Ivit ad Hibernos Sophia mirabile claros.
(*A Prospect of the State of Ireland*, pp 56–7).

A near-contemporary translation of the lines reads:

The fathers old he following, for love to read good works,
Went unto Irish men, who were (O wonder) famous Clarkes.
(William Camden, *Britain*, trans. Philémon Holland [2nd ed. London, 1637], 'Hibernia: Ireland', p. 68).

Sulgenus is the Latinized name of Sulien (*c.*1012–91), bishop of St David's in Wales. His son Ieuan made a copy of St Augustine's *De trinitate* concluding with the Latin verses, 'Ieuan's poem on the life and family of Sulien', that include the lines quoted by Walsh and Butler.

p. 40 *Four Great Universities in Ireland*: Butler's source is once more Peter Walsh's *A Prospect of the State of Ireland*: 'Besides all the Irish Chronicles tell us of the four great Universities in *Ireland*, *Ardmagh*, *Cashel*, *Dun-da-Leathglass*, and *Lismore*' (*Prospect*, p. 57); Walsh attributes this information to Keating (*General History*, p. 424).

p. 40 *Keting*: i.e. Keating.

p. 40 *Couchuvair Mac-Donochoe ... 7000 Scholars*: Butler continues to quote from Walsh, *Prospect*, p. 57.

p. 40 *Paris and Pavia*: Again, Butler follows Walsh, *Prospect*, p. 57.

p. 40 *Spenser in his View of Ireland, page 29*: Edmund Spenser (1552?–99) was both a poet and author of *A View of the Present State of Ireland* (written 1596; published 1633). The passage to which Butler refers is:

> *Irenæus*. ... it is certaine, that Ireland hath had the use of letters very anciently, and long before *England* ... that they had letters aunciently, is nothing doubtfull, for the *Saxons of England* are said to have their letters, & learning, and learned men from the *Irish*, and that also appeareth by the likenesse of the Character, for the *Saxons* Character is the same with the Irish.

A View of the State of Ireland, in *The Historie of Ireland, collected by three learned authors, viz. Meredith Hanmer Doctor in Divinitie: Edmund Campion sometime Fellow of St. Johns Colledge in Oxford: and Edmund Spenser, Esq*. [Dublin, 1633], pp 29–30), but her source was most probably Walsh, *Prospect*, p. 58.

pp 40–1 *Bede, Camden, Heylin, Spenser, Hanmor, Campion, Dr. Keting, Sir James Ware, Flahertus, and P. Walsh*: Bede (see n. to p. 40 above); Camden (see n. to p. 40 above); *Heylin*: Peter Heylin, or Heylyn (1599–1662), English clergyman and historian, mentioned here for his *Cosmographie* (1652); *Spenser* (see n. to p. 40 above); *Hanmor*: Meredith Hanmer (1543–1604), English-born Church of Ireland clergyman, author of *A Chronicle of Ireland*, edited by Daniel Molyneux, Ulster King of Arms, and published along with works by Spenser and Campion, by Sir James Ware in 1633; *Campion*: St Edmund Campion (1540–81), English-born Jesuit, martyred at Tyburn in London, author of *History of Ireland*, published by James Ware in the same 1633 collection as histories by Spenser and Hanmer; *Sir James Ware*: Ware (1594–1666), Dublin-born antiquarian and historian who brought together three important sixteenth-century English accounts of Ireland, by Hanmer, Campion, and Spenser, in a volume entitled *The Historie of Ireland* (Dublin, 1633); *Flahertus*: Roderic O'Flaherty, or Ruaidhrí Óg Ó Flaithbheartaigh (1627x30–1716x18), Irish historian, author whose Latin *Ogygia; seu, Rerum Hibernicarum chronologia* (1685) was based on Irish-language manuscript sources.

p. 41 *I have ... omitted ... Twenty four of the Twenty five Battles which Bryan Boraimh Fought in his Reign and won*: *Bryan Boraimh*: Brian Bóruma or Brian Boru (*c*.941–1014), king of Munster and later high-king of Ireland from 1002 until his death at the Battle of Clontarf (though in the chronology of *Foras Feasa ar Éirinn*, Keating has him take possession of the throne of Ireland in 1027 [*General History*, p. 496]). In her reference to the twenty-five battles, Butler follows Keating:

> This martial and renown'd Prince *Bryen Boiroimhe* King of *Munster*, was an Instrument in the Hand of Providence, to scourge the Insolence and

> Cruelty of those Foreigners, which he did successfully, for he routed them in twenty five Battels, from the first Time he enter'd the Field against them to the last Conflict he had with them, which was the Battel of *Cluaintarf*, where he was slain, being then possess'd of the Government of the Island. (*General History*, p. 483).

See also 'Appendix 1: List of names'.

p. 41 *half so many Score*: Butler, in fact, condenses over a century of Irish history, rather than 40 or 50 years. It should be noted, however, that Butler was not unique in this approach to historical fiction. Jane Barker, for instance, wrote in the preface to *Exilius* (London, 1715): 'As to the Historical Part, I suppose the Reader does not expect much Exactness, it being a Romance, not an History; so it matters not who, or who, were Co-temporaries, but there having been such, and such Names, and Families, one may reasonably suppose that some of the Children or Branches of those Families, flourish'd all at the same time, which is sufficient to vindicate the Book in that Point from extream Absurdity' (p. [ix]).

p. 41 *I have constrain'd my self ... to make my Lovers die unmarried*: Far from being constrained by her source material in Keating and others, Butler performs the radical excision of more than a century of Irish history in the interests of her narrative of Irish resistance to foreign aggression; she is equally bold in writing a romance in which, very unexpectedly for the time, the virtuous lovers do not find the happy ending the romance narrative implies.

p. 41 *Turgesius*: Turges, sometimes Thorgest or Thorgils (d. 845), a Viking leader who established a fleet on Lough Ree (see n. to p. 43 below), and plundered the surrounding areas, destroying monasteries at Clonmacnoise, Clonfert and Lough Derg, among others. Keating, who refers to him as the Danish 'Usurper' (*General History*, p. 432), drew his account largely from the early-twelfth century *Cogadh Gaedel re Gaillaibh*, supplemented by an episode recounted in *The Topography of Ireland* by Gerald of Wales. See also 'Appendix 1: List of names'.

p. 41 *the Beauty of a Virgin*: Butler seems here to glance at the *aisling* (Irish: dream), a poetic genre in which Ireland appears in a vision in the form of a young (sometimes old) woman, who foretells a revival of Irish fortunes. The *aisling* was developed by Aogán Ó Rathaille, or Egan O'Rahilly (1675–1729), and was originally a poetic form associated with Jacobitism, foretelling the return of the Stuarts, as does *Irish Tales* itself.

p. 43 *bloody Wars ... against the powerful Danes*: The invaders from present-day Denmark and Norway, also called Vikings, Norsemen, or Ostmen, raided Britain and Ireland from the end of the eighth century until the middle of the tenth century, by which time many had settled in the lands they had once attacked; although they suffered some early defeats, they were especially active in Ireland in the 830s and 840s. In the *General History*, Keating writes of the Danes that 'those Foreigners, who made an Attempt upon the Island at that Time, were Natives of the Kingdom of *Dania* of *Denmark*, and these People are call'd in the old *Irish* Records by the Name of *Dubhgeinte* or *Dubh Lochlannuig*', contrasting them with the Norwegians 'who came originally from *Norway* ... stiled in the Chronicles *Finngeinte* or *Fionn Lochlannaig* (p. 418). That Sarah Butler consistently refers to these invaders as 'Danes' may reflect the influence of Keating but also serves to remind readers that the army of the protestant William III that defeated the forces of the catholic James II in 1689–91 contained a large number of Danish mercenaries.

p. 43 *Turgesius*: See n. to p. 41 above, and 'Appendix 1: List of Names'.

p. 43 *Lough-Ribh*: Lough Ree, one of the three lakes on the river Shannon.

p. 43 *Athlone*: Situated on the Shannon at the foot of Lough Ree, close to the geographical centre of Ireland, in the present-day Co. Westmeath.

p. 44 *Garrison*: The Danes did establish garrisons in Ireland. However, following the Williamite victory, the British army – an exclusively protestant and largely English force after 1701 – also made extensive efforts to garrison Ireland, so that by the mid-eighteenth century it had garrison towns in Cork, Limerick, Galway, Waterford and Kinsale, as well as Dublin, which boasted the largest garrison outside those of Gibraltar and Minorca, at a time when Great Britain was at war with Spain; see Alan J. Guy, 'The Irish military establishment, 1660–1776', in Thomas Bartlett and Keith Jeffery (eds), *A Military History of Ireland* (Cambridge: Cambridge University Press, 1996), p. 222. See also Keating's 'A particular ACCOUNT *of the* SLAVERY *imposed upon the ancient* Irish *by* TURGESIUS *the* Danish *Tyrant*', *General History*, pp 432 ff.

p. 44 *Dooneflaith, the Daughter of Maolsechelvin King of Meath*: For Dooneflaith and Maolseachelvin, see n. to p. 39 above, and 'Appendix 1: Index to Names'. In addition to the high-kingship of Ireland, for which there is evidence from at least the ninth century, there existed various provincial kingships, including those of Leinster, Connacht, Munster, and those of the Southern Uí Néill or Mide (Meath) and the Northern Uí Néill or Aileach.

p. 44 *Prince Murchoe*: See n. to p. 39 above, and 'Appendix 1: List of Names'.

p. 44 *Bryan Boriamh*: See n. to p. 41 above, and 'Appendix 1: List of Names'; in *Irish Tales*, the names are variously spelled: Brian and Bryan; Boriamh and Boraimhe.

p. 44 *Elected King of all Ireland*: Seventeenth-century Irish readings of Keating laid emphasis on the supposedly harmonious relationship between king and people that existed in early Ireland, with monarch and parliament acting for the general good of the country.

p. 47 *Capitulations*: Agreements or stipulations.

p. 47 *all his Pagan Gods*: Ireland had been evangelized by the fifth century; the Viking invaders, by contrast, were pagans. The general profession of Christianity in Scandinavia did not take place until after the events described in *Irish Tales*, though some Viking settlers converted to Christianity in Ireland as part of a wider process of acculturation.

p. 48 *I shall but take into my Bosom a Snake*: Proverbial by the eighteenth century, the phrase derives from the fable by Aesop (sixth century BC) concerning a farmer who, taking pity on a frozen snake, warms it in his bosom, only to be fatally bitten when the snake revives.

p. 49 *an Harp*: The harp frequently mentioned by Keating in *Foras Feasa*, would have been the *crott*, a harp-like instrument for which sources exist at least from the eighth century; the *cláirseach*, or Irish harp, dates from no earlier than the twelfth century, with the oldest extant example, popularly known as the 'Brian Boru' harp (held in the Library of Trinity College Dublin), dating from the fifteenth century.

p. 50 *puissant*: Mighty, powerful.

p. 51 *currant*: i.e. current.

p. 52 *Yoak*: i.e. yoke.

p. 53 *loose*: i.e. lose.

p. 56 *Buckler*: Shield.

p. 57 *Armagh*: Already an important religious site during the pre-Christian era in Ireland (Ard Mhacha = the Height of Macha, a pagan goddess), Armagh was supposedly refounded by St. Patrick in 457, according to *Annals of the Four Masters*, becoming, as it remains, the ecclesiastical capital of Ireland, for the Roman Catholic church and the protestant Church of Ireland alike.

p. 59 *suddain*: i.e. sudden.

p. 61 *Banes*: i.e. banns.

p. 61 *reaking*: i.e. reeking.

p. 64 *Pander*: Procurer; from Pandarus, the Trojan soldier who procured the love of Cressida for Troilus, in Boccaccio's *Il Filostrato* (1335) and Chaucer's *Troilus and Criseyde* (late 1380s?).

p. 65 *No Lustful Heat … forgive the rest*: The lines seem to be the work of the author.

p. 67 *Fourteen Youths … all clad and dress'd like thee*: Different versions of this story, related by Keating (*General History*, pp 436–9), are told by many authors, including Raphael Holinshed in his *Chronicles* (2nd ed. London, 1586), 'The First Inhabitants of Ireland', II, p. 56 and Heylin, *Cosmographie* (1652), 'Ireland', I, p. 312, but the story appears to originate with Gerald of Wales.

p. 68 *Treatment*: Entertainment, banquet.

p. 69 *Alexander … Euphrates*: The story of the purported meeting between Alexander the Great and Thalestris, Queen of the Amazons, who hoped the Macedonian king would father her children and those of her 300 Amazons, is told in an unhistorical Greek romance, and was dismissed as fiction by Plutarch (*c*.46–120) in his *Life of Alexander*.

p. 69 *Mars*: Roman god of war.

p. 69 *Venus*: Roman goddess of love and fertility.

p. 72 *Bacchus's Battles*: i.e. drinking; Bacchus was the Roman god of wine.

p. 72 *Centaurs*: In Greek myth, the Centaurs, half-man, half-horse, inhabited Mount Pelion in Thessaly. Butler alludes to the wedding feast of the Lapith king, Pirithous, to which his former enemies, the Centaurs, had been invited; unused to drinking wine, the Centaur Eurytion attempted to rape the bride, Hypodamia, causing King Theseus to intervene, with the result that the centaurs were killed or injured, and expelled from Thessaly. The story, known as the centauromachy, is represented on the metopes of the Parthenon in Athens.

p. 73 *River Laugh-Ainme*: Lough Ainme (in Keating, Lough Aininn) or Ennell is near Mullingar, in the present Co. Westmeath. The story that Turgesius was killed by being bound and drowned is directly at odds with the account given by Gerald of Wales that he was killed by Prince Murchad and the disguised warriors, but is credited by modern historians, based on the annalistic evidence.

p. 74 *Minion*: Here, a derogatory term for a lover.

p. 75 *Doom*: Judgment, sentence.

p. 78 *Election of the Princes and Nobility of Ireland*: The reference here is to Máel Sechnaill mac Máele Ruanaid Uí Néill, also known as Máel Sechnaill I, king of Meath and later High King of Ireland (d. 862). Keating similarly emphasizes the 'election' of the king, declaring that '*Maolseachlin*, by the Suffrage of the Nobility and Gentry, was placed upon the Throne of *Ireland*' (*General History*, p. 440).

p. 78 *Amelanus, Cytaracus, and Ivorus*: Butler again follows Keating closely here, though with characteristic variation in the spelling of proper names: '*After the Death of* Turgesius, *three Brothers*, Amelanus, Cyracus, *and* Imorus, *came from the Parts of* Norway *in a peaceable Manner, and under Pretence of Merchandising, arrived with their Followers in this Island*' (*General History*, p. 441).

p. 79 *Oostmans*: More usually Oostmen or Ostmen; a name given to Norsemen who invaded Ireland in the tenth century and settled on the east coast of the country.

p. 79 *the Irish were forc'd once more to have recourse to their Arms*: It is at this point that Butler collapses her source material from Keating in order to produce a simpler, more powerful narrative of Irish resistance to foreign invasion and tyrannic rule (see also 'Introduction', pp 25–7). Keating's account emphasizes Irish responsibility for their renewed political defeat: 'But the greatest Advantages that were given to [the Invaders] by the Natives, were occasion'd by the Contests and civil Discords among themselves; nothing promoted the common Ruin more than their Animosities within themselves, and their unnatural and irreconcilable Quarrels were attended with more dreadful Effects, than could follow from all the Force of the Enemy … Thus were the unfortunate *Irish*, by a Concurrence of unhappy Circumstances, again oblig'd to pass under the Yoke, which gall'd them with inexpressible Misery, and could never be shaken off till the Death of that illustrious Hero, the brave *Bryen Boiroimhne*, King of *Ireland*' (*General History*, p. 442).

p. 79 *Maolsechelvin's Heart ... Murchoe should marry his Daughter*: From this point onwards, the Maolsechelvin referred to is Máel Sechnaill mac Domnaill, or Máel Seachnaill II (d. 1022), the great-great grandson of Máel Sechnaill I (see n. to p. 78, 'Election ... Princes', above). Máel Sechnaill II was deposed as high king of Ireland by Brian Boru in 1002 but once more took the throne following the latter's death at the battle of Clontarf in 1014. Butler has ingeniously compacted her narrative by omitting over 100 years of Irish history characterized, according to her source, by internecine warfare.

p. 80 *Tomond*: Brian Boru was son of Cennétig (d. 951), king of Tuadmumu, or Thomond (in north Munster).

p. 82 *Murchoe ... Cean-Choradh*: Butler's immediate inspiration for this passage seems to be Keating's reference to the military exploits of Murchoe (Murchad) leading to the capture of an enemy king whom he carries prisoner to Cean Coradh [Kincora in Co. Clare]. However, the following account of Murchoe's lovesickness for Dooneflaith constrasts strikingly with Keating who immediately continues by relating that '*Mortough* the Son of the King of *Ireland*, a valiant and warlike Prince, enter'd the Province of *Leinster* with Fire and Sword, and raged over the Country in a terrible Manner as far as *Gleanda Loch* [Glendalough in Co. Wicklow], and from thence he led his victorious Army to *Kilmainham*' (*General History*, p. 497). Keating later offers an account, extended over several folio pages, of Brian Boru's style of living at Kincora: 'This magnificent Prince supported his royal Grandeur by a splendid Court, and kept a most sumptuous and hospitable Table suited to his Dignity ...' (*General History*, p. 500).

p. 84 *Twenty five bloody pitch'd Battles*: See n. to p. 41 above.

p. 84 *Dublin, Weixford, Waterford, Cork, or Limerick*: Butler follows Keating once more: 'It must be observ'd ... that *Bryen Boiroimhe*, King of *Ireland*, had so much at Heart the Honour of his Country, that by his Authority he expell'd all the *Danes* throughout the Island, except such as inhabited the Cities of *Dublin*, *Wexford*, *Waterford*, *Cork*, and *Limerick*, whom he permitted to remain in the Country for the Benefit of Trade; for these Foreigners were a mercantile People, and by Importation supplied the Kingdom with Commodities that serv'd both for Pleasure and Use, and by this Means were a publick Advantage to the whole Nation' (p. 505).

p. 85 *Maolmordh Mac Murchoe*: Máel Mórda, son of Murchad mac Finn, king of Leinster. See also 'Appendix 1: List of names'.

p. 85 *Garmlaigh*: Gormlaith (d. 1030), wife to, successively, Óláfr Sihtricson, Brian Boru, and Máel Sechnaill II. See also 'Appendix 1: List of names'.

p. 85 *Linster*: i.e. Leinster.

p. 86 *a Nobleman and Murchoe playing a Game at Chess*: Butler takes the following story from Keating, *General History*, p. 504.

p. 86 *Gleaun Mama*: The Battle of Glen Máma (Keating: Gleann Madmha), or the Glen of the Gap, was fought in 999, possibly in present-day Co. Wicklow, and formed part of the Leinster revolt against Brian Boru, who joined with King Máel Sechnaill, their combined armies defeating the forces of Leinster and Dublin.

p. 86 *jear*: i.e. jeer.

p. 87 *Lyon*: i.e. lion.

p. 87 *the chief of the Danes*: Sihtric or Sigtryggr Óláfsson (d. 1042), also known as Sigtryggr Silkiskegg or Sihtric Silkbeard. Sihtric was the son of Gormlaith (see 'Appendix 1: List of Names') and Óláfr Sihtricson and had become King of Dublin in 989, later fighting alongside Máel Sechnaill II at the Battle of Glen Máma (see n. to p. 86 above). Subsequently loyal to Brian Boru, he mounted a renewed challenge to his authority in 1013, seeking help from other Viking settlements in the north of England, the Isle of Man, the Hebrides and Orkney.

p. 87 *the king of Denmark*: The king of Denmark at the time was Svend Tveskegg or Sweyn Forkbeard (r. 986/7–1014); however, Sihtric's appeal for assistance in his struggle against Brian Boru was made, most importantly, to Sigurd, earl of Orkney, who lost his life at the Battle of Clontarf in 1014.

p. 87 *hast*: i.e. haste.

p. 87 *Carolus Knutus, and Andreas his Brother*: Here, Butler follows Keating who, in Dermod O'Connor's translation, identifies the sons of the king of Denmark as Carolus Cnutus and Andrew (*General History*, p. 506), and records that both were killed at Clontarf. However, Knut, or Canute (d. 1035) became king of England in 1016, while the identification of Andreas is unclear (Knut's only known brother being Harald).

p. 87 *twelve thousand Danes*: Butler follows her source closely here, this being the figure given by Keating; see *General History*, p. 506.

p. 87 *Clantarf*: i.e. Clontarf (see following note).

p. 90 *Clantarfe*: The battle of Clontarf (*Cath Chluain Tarbh*), just outside of Dublin, took place in 1014 (1034 in Keating's chronology). Despite the fact that his army was outnumbered by the combined might of the Dublin and Leinster armies, reinforced by troops from the western and northern isles and the Isle of Man, Brian Boru won the day, though both he and his son, Murchad, were among those killed.

p. 90 *Magnealta*: Butler follows Keating: '*Bryen Boiroimhe* began to march, and directed his Course to the Plains of *Magh Nealta*, where they found the King of *Leinster* and the *Danish* Forces, expecting his Arrival' (*General History*, p. 507); Mágh nEalta, anglicized as Moynalty, was originally the name given to the large area lying between today's Tallaght, Clontarf and the Howth peninsula.

p. 90 *Good Friday*: The battle of Clontarf was fought on Good Friday, 23 April 1014.

p. 91 *fourscore and eight*: This is the age given by Keating (*General History*, p. 509); modern historians believe that Brian Boru was in his early-to-mid 70s when he was killed.

p. 92 *Bruador*: Butler follows Keating's account here: 'a Body of these Foreigners in their Flight chanc'd to pass by the royal Pavilion of the King, which when they understood, they enter'd under the Leading of *Bruadar* that was the Captain of those Runaways, and finding the King of *Ireland*, they drew upon him and slew him; but the Death of this Monarch was soon reveng'd by the *Irish* Guards, who coming into the Tent, and seeing the King dead upon the Ground, fell upon *Bruadar* and his cowardly *Danes* and cut them all to Pieces' (*General History*, p. 508). Bruadar, or Brodir, is named as Boru's killer in the Iceland saga *Njála*.

p. 93 *seven petty Kings*: Butler paraphrases rather than quotes the losses incurred by Brian Boru's army, though Keating does mention seven kings by name (*General History*, pp 508–9).

p. 93 *Maolseachelvin, (who now the second time sat on the Monarchical Throne of Ireland)*: Máel Sechnaill II both preceded and succeeded Brian Boru as high-king; see 'Appendix 1: List of names'.

p. 93 *Huaghaire Mac-Duniling Mac-Tuatil*: In his translation of Keating, Dermod O'Connor renders this name as '*Ungaire* the son of *Dunlaing*'; see *General History*, p. 515.

p. 93 *Stetirick the Son of Aomlaibh*: In Keating, '*Sitric* the Son of *Humphry*' (*General History*, p. 515); i.e. Sihtric (see n. to p. 87 above), son of Óláfr Sigtriggsson, known in Irish as Amlaíb Cúarán

List of emendations

The present text respects the spelling and punctuation of the first edition of *Irish Tales*, with the exception only of the emendations noted below, and of the conventions used to denote direct speech; here, the running quotations marks in the left-hand margin, characteristic of eighteenth-century printing, have been replaced by a single quotation mark at the beginning and end of each passage of direct speech.

p. 33: VIII.] VIII
p. 40, l. 9: claros] daros
p. 40, l. 15: than] that
p. 52, l. 11: Maolseachelvin] Moalseachelvin
p. 52, l. 14: Maolseachelvin] Moalseachelvin
p. 54, l. 12: think] thing
p. 58, l. 12up: waited a] wait-a
p. 62, l. 7: affliction] afflicton
p. 62, l. 6up: Maolseachelvin] Moalseachelvin
p. 63, ll. 7–8up: he is resolv'd to have you – his Mistress'. Reply'd *Dooneflaith* hastily] he is resolv'd to have you – his Mistress, reply'd *Dooneflaith* hastily
p. 65, l. 2: Heart'.] Heart',
p. 66, l. 5up: Generous] Genereus
p. 70, l. 4up: Commanders] Commaners
p. 72, l. 12: Fate.] Fate,
p. 73, l. 7: Christianity] Christianty
p. 73, l. 18: there] their
p. 78, l. 6: you] you you
p. 81, l. 15up: Crown,] Crown.
p. 85, l. 12up: *Tomond*] *Tomad*
p. 88, l. 7up: to see] too see

Appendix 1: List of names

Throughout *Irish Tales*, Irish proper names appear in inconsistent and sometimes eccentric form, even for an age when English orthography was not as fixed as it would later become. In part, the inconsistency and apparent eccentricity almost certainly result from a combination of the unfamiliarity of these Irish names to English eyes, and to misreadings of the authorial manuscript by the compositors working for the booksellers. While obvious errors have been corrected (see 'List of emendations', p. 110), the names have otherwise been left as they appear, since no attempt at regularization is possible, short of modernizing the entire text. The unusual forms of names and their inconsistent printing indicate in fact just how unfamiliar the Irish historical material was to an English audience. In order to help modern readers, the following index distinguishes between names in the form(s) given by Sarah Butler, those used by Dermod O'Connor in his translation of Seathrún Céitinn's *Foras Feasa ar Éirinn*, written in Irish *c.*1634 but first published in English, as *The General History of Ireland* (London, 1723), by Peter Walsh, *A Prospect of the State of Ireland from the year of the world 1750, to the year of Christ 1652* (London, 1682), and those used by modern historians. For the dates of birth and death, we have followed those suggested in the *Oxford Dictionary of National Biography*.

Bryan Boraimh: Brian Boru, or Brian Bóruma (c. 941–1014), king of Munster after 978, and high-king (*ard-rí*) of Ireland from 1002. Dermod O'Connor's translation of *Foras Feasa ar Éirinn* uses the form Bryen Boiroimhe and Keating provides a genealogy for the king: 'He was the Son of *Kennedy*, Son of *Lorcan*, Son of *Lachtna*, Son of *Cathal*, Son of *Corc*, Son of *Anluan*, Son of *Mahon*, Son of *Turlagh*, Son of *Cathol*, Son of *Hugh Caomh*, Son of *Eoichaidh Baldearg*, Son of *Carthan Fionn*, Son of *Bloin*, Son of *Cais*, Son of *Conall Eachlauth*, Son of *Luighdheach Meann*, Son of *Aongus Tireach*, Son of *Firchuirb*, Son of *Modha Chuirb*, Son of *Cormac Cas,* Son of *Oiliolla Olum*, descended from the royal Line of *Heber Fionn*, and govern'd the Kingdom twelve Years'; Jeoffry Keating, *The General History of Ireland*, trans. Dermo'd [sic] O Connor (London, 1723), p. 496.

Dooneflaith: The name given to the daughter of 'Maolseachelvin' – Máel Sechnaill I – by Sarah Butler, who justifies her choice at some length (see 'Preface', p. 39 above). Dooneflaith is certainly an appropriate name for the heroine of *Irish Tales*, as the first element, *donn*, denotes brown, a colour associated with the ancient Irish nobility, while the second element, *flaith*, denotes sovereignty and was hence associated with royal blood. How much of this Sarah Butler knew is uncertain, however, for she demonstrably both misremembered and adapted her source material in Keating, who records 'Dunflath' as being the mother of Máel Sechnaill II: '*Maolseachluin* was the succeeding Monarch; He was the Son of *Flann Sionna* ... The Mother of this Monarch was *Dunflath* the Daughter of *Mortough Mac Neill*' (*General History*, p. 486).

Garmlaigh: (Keating: Gorm Fhlath) Gormlaith (d. 1030), wife of Brian Boru, and Queen of Ireland. One of Brian's several wives, Gormlaith was not mother to his son Murchad. She had herself previously been married to Óláfr Sihtricson, and after Brian's death married his successor, Máel Sechnaill mac Domnaill, Máel Sechnaill II. Like Dooneflaith, the name Gormlaith was associated with female royal blood.

Maolmordh Mac Murchoe: (Keating: Maolmordha), Máel Mórda, son of Murchad mac Finn, king of Leinster (966–72); he was brother to Gormlaith (Keating: Gorm Fhlath) or Garmlaigh, in Butler's transcription, wife to Brian Boru.

Maolseachelvin: An eccentric spelling, probably resulting from an English compositor's misreading of the manuscript's 'Maolseachluin': i.e. Maelsechlainn or Máel Sechnaill. In *Irish Tales*, Maolseachelvin is a composite character: a conflation of (1) Máel Sechnaill mac Máele Ruanaid Uí Néill (d. 862), king of Mide, and high-king or *ard-rí* of Ireland, 846–62, and (2) Máel Sechnaill mac Domnaill (948–1022), king of Mide, and high-king of Ireland 980–1002 and again from 1014–22.

Murchoe: (Keating: Morrough; Walsh: Murchoe) Murchad (d. 1014), son of Brian Boru by his first wife, Mór. Murchad was killed, along with his father, at the Battle of Clontarf. In *Irish Tales* Murchoe is unmarried and in love with Dooneflaith; yet while Keating does not mention the prince's marriage, his account of the Battle of Clontarf includes a passage indicating that '*Morrough* the Prince of *Ireland* was resolv'd to distinguish himself in this Expedition, and took with him his Son *Turlough* and his five Brothers, *Teige*, *Donough*, *Daniel*, *Connor* and *Flann* (p. 506), suggesting a rather different narrative from the one offered by Butler. In having Murchad killed at Clontarf, Butler follows her principal source, Keating (*General History*, p. 508); Keating's own primary source for the battle was the early-twelfth century *Cogadh Gaedel re Gaillaibh*. Another of Butler's sources, Peter Walsh, writes: 'immediately after this Battel of *Clantarff* ... the Victorious Army of *Brian Boraimh* had buried their dead (especially this Monarch himself and *Murchoe* the Prince his eldest Son ...)', Peter Walsh, *A Prospect of the State of Ireland* (London, 1682), pp 162–3.

Turgesius: Turges, sometimes Thorgest or Thorgils (d. 845), a Viking leader who established a fleet on Lough Ree (see n. to p. 43 above), and plundered the surrounding areas, destroying monasteries at Clonmacnoise, Clonfert and Lough Derg, among others. The story of Maél Sechnaill's ploy that leads to Turges's death derives from Gerald of Wales (Giraldus Cambrensis), *Topography of Ireland*, III, chap. xl: 'Turgesius happened at the time to be very much enamoured of the daughter of Omachlachlienus, the king of Meath. The king hid his hatred in his heart, and granting the girl to Turgesius, promised to send her to him with fifteen beautiful maidens to a certain island in Meath, in the lake of Lochver. Turgesius was delighted and went to the rendezvous on the appointed day with fifteen nobles of his people. They encountered on the island, decked out in girls' clothes to practise their deceit, fifteen young men, shaven of their beards, full of spirit, and especially picked for the job. They carried knives hidden on their persons, and with these they killed Turgesius and his companions in the midst of their embraces', *The History and Topography of Ireland*, trans. John J. O'Meara (rev. ed. Mountrath: Dolmen Press, 1982), pp 120–1. For her conclusion of the episode, Butler follows Keating, who relates the conflicting story that Turgesius was spared in the general slaughter and later drowned in Lough Aininn (Lough Ennell).

Appendix 2: William Philips, *Hibernia Freed* (1722), and the dramatic uses of Irish history

Given the complexity of the political and cultural moment in Ireland, following the 1715 Jacobite Rebellion, it is perhaps unsurprising that few writers of imaginative literature sought to follow the lead of Sarah Butler in her use of ancient history in *Irish Tales*. The closest counterpart to the novel, in the decade that followed, is William Philips's *Hibernia Freed* (1722), a tragedy first performed at the Theatre Royal in Lincoln's Inn Fields in London.[1] Irish history of a later period was also used – to very different effect – by the near contemporary play, *Rotherick O'Connor* by Charles Shadwell.

Like Butler's novel, *Hibernia Freed: A Tragedy* embodies an account of Irish history characterized by invasion. William Philips was both Irish and a Jacobite. The dedication he wrote was, unlike that of Charles Gildon, more plausibly addressed not to a Hanoverian Whig nobleman but to an Irish aristocrat of Gaelic descent: Henry O'Brien, earl of Thomond, one of whose ancestors, O Brien, king of Ulster, is the hero of the tragedy. While the earl of Thomond had recently accepted a British peerage – becoming Viscount Tadcaster in 1713 – his continuing attachment to Ireland is invoked in Philips's assertion that 'As Love of my Country induced me to lay the Scene of a Play there; so the particular Honour I bear to, and ought to have for, Your Lordship's Family, oblig'd me to search for a Story, in which one of Your Lordship's Ancestors made so noble a Figure; for what is so noble as to free ones Country from Tyranny and Invasion'.[2]

Written, as Philips declared, 'in Praise of my Country', *Hibernia Freed* opens on the 'Hill of Tarah', before the tent of O Brien, 'Monarch of *Ireland*', who bewails his country's fate, along with his own, since 'Fatal Disunion and intestine Strife/Have render'd us a Prey to foreign Pow'r' (Act 1, sc. 1; p. 2) The

1 It is uncertain whether *Hibernia Freed* was ever performed in Dublin; for evidence of a performance at the Smock Alley theatre on 31 March 1722, see Helen M. Burke, *Riotous Performances: The Struggle for Hegemony in the Irish Theatre, 1712–1784* (Notre Dame, IN: University of Notre Dame Press, 2003), p. 301, n. 3.

2 William Philips, *Hibernia Freed* (London, 1722), p. 2. Further references are given parenthetically in the text; the dedication and the unlineated text are separately paginated.

invitation to understand the drama as parallel history is so insistent that it could hardly have been overlooked by the most casual reader, as when O Brien apostrophizes the River Boyne, no longer the source of fruitfulness, declaiming (in terms, if not tones, familiar from much contemporary political writing):

> Fertile *Hibernia!* Hospitable Land!
> Is not allow'd to feed her Native Sons,
> In vain they toil, and a-mid Plenty starve.
> The lazy *Dane* grows wanton with our Stores,
> Urges our Labour, and derides our Wants (Act I, sc. 1; p. 3).

If this is the present, then the past is similarly evoked:

> *Hibernia!* Seat of Learning! School of Science!
> How waste! How wild dost thou already seem!
> Thy Houses, Schools, thy Cities ransack'd, burnt! (Act I, sc. 1; p. 3).

Hibernia Freed is not a good play but it is one that makes its patriotic and political values clear. The climax of the tragedy dramatizes a version of the killing of Turgesius by fifteen armed warriors disguised as maidens, though here with the added irony (not present in any source but invented by Philips) that it is Turgesius who stipulates the number of women who shall accompany the king of Ireland's daughter, Sabina, whom Turgesius treacherously pretends to court but whom he designs to give over to his henchman, Erric 'the Ravisher'. In *Hibernia Freed*, it is O Neill, king of Ulster – rather than Murchoe – who is caught between the competing calls of patriotic duty and love: in his case for Agnes, daughter of Herimon, who is also the object of the arrogant desire of Turgesius. It is Erric, who declares himself in love with Agnes, who most clearly reveals the tyrannical behaviour of the Danes, attempting to threaten Agnes, by emphasizing the destructive potential of the enemy forces: 'Should I command, thy Nation is no more' (II, 1; p. 16). In the final act, the Danes are, of course, defeated but Turgesius's final words, as he is led to execution, sound a cautionary note:

> But e'er I part, remember I foretell,
> Another Nation shall revenge my Death,
> And with successful Arms invade this Realm. (Act V, sc. 1; p. 57)

Conscious that this prediction must include not only the Norman, Elizabethan and Cromwellian but also the Williamite invasion of Ireland, Philips perhaps thought it prudent to interpolate a speech by the bard Eugenius who, divinely inspired, declares:

Another Nation shall indeed succeed,
But different far in Manners from the *Dane*.
(So Heav'n inspires and urges me to speak)
Another Nation, famous through the World,
For martial Deeds, for strength and Skill in Arms,
Belov'd and blest for their Humanity.
Where Wealth abounds, and Liberty resides,
Where Learning ever shall maintain her Seat,
And Arts and Sciences shall flourish ever.
Of gen'rous Minds and honourable Blood;
Goodly the Men, the Women heav'nly fair,
The happy Parents of a happy Race,
They shall succeed, invited to our Aid,
And mix their Blood with ours; one People grow,
Polish our Manners, and improve our Minds. (Act V, sc. 1; p. 57)

The effect of this transparent eulogy of England is considerably undermined, however, by the immediately following words spoken by O Brien, which conclude the drama:

Whatever Changes are decreed by Fate,
Bear we with Patience, with a Will resign'd. (Act V, sc. 1; p. 57)

If, more cautious than Butler, William Philips bore the post-Williamite settlement in Ireland with patience and a will resigned, another contemporary chose to emphasize instead the 'common naturalization',[3] in a later-eighteenth century phrase, that would make the Irish and the English 'one people grow'.

Charles Shadwell's *Rotherick O'Connor, King of Connaught; or, The Distress'd Princess* (1720), was performed in the Smock Alley theatre in the 1719–20 season. It was in 1720 that the hotly-debated Declaratory Act, which followed Poyning's Law in subordinating the Irish parliament to the parliament at Westminster, came into force. Shadwell's tragedy, set at the time of the invasion of Ireland by Richard de Clare, earl of Pembroke, known as Strongbow, was patently aimed at reconciling a Dublin audience to the provisions of the new Act.[4] Besides the

3 [Edmund Burke], *A Letter to the Right Honourable Henry Grattan, on the proposed tax on absentees* ([Dublin] 1792?), p. 9.

4 Shadwell's 'Prologue' reflects pertinently on the Irish nature of his material: 'From distant Clime, each scribbling Author brings,/A Race of *Heroes*, and a Race of *Kings*;/And in soft Numbers humbly does implore,/To Act his Murders, on this boarded Floor,/His Rebels, Virgins, *Heroes*, all must Dye,/To grace some Conqueror in his Tragedy./Be he a *Roman*, *Greek*, or *Persian* Born,/Thus Forreign Stories, do our Stage Adorn./Our Author tries, by Different Ways to please,/And shews you Kings, That never cross'd the Seas', 'Prologue, spoke by Mr. Gifford. Written by Mr. Shadwell', *The Works of Mr. Charles Shadwell* (Dublin,

eponymous protagonist, other characters include Dermot MacMurrough (Diarmait Mac Murchada) and Eva (Aoife), his daughter, whom Strongbow marries: the event that Daniel Maclise would make the subject of one of the most famous of all nineteenth-century Irish historical paintings: *The Marriage of Strongbow and Aoife* (1854), now in the National Gallery of Ireland.[5]

In marked contrast to Philips's later Jacobite treatment of the Turgesius story, Shadwell's *Rotherick O'Connor* offers an explicitly Hanoverian, and anti-Jacobite, drama, in which Eva quickly hails Henry II as that 'Godlike Man' and whose political values are encapsulated in the closing words of Shadwell's 'Prologue':

> Learn then from those unhappy Days of Yore,
> To scorn and hate an Arbitrary Power.
> To Praise and Love those Laws that make you Free,
> And are the Great Bullworks of your Liberty
> Adore the Prince who rules by milder Sway,
> And like good Subjects, Lawfully Obey:
> All Tragedies this Moral shou'd Observe,
> The best of Kings does surely best Deserve (p. 267).

Here, the 'best of Kings' – a conflation of Henry II, William III, and George I – is opposed to James II or the Old Pretender, whose designs are for 'Arbitrary Sway'. Shadwell's use of Irish history would seem, in the words of Helen M. Burke, unequivocally to reinvent 'English hegemony in Ireland'. Even so, a degree of ambivalence remains, and the play's triumphalism is defused, for while Strongbow tells Eva that 'I've sav'd your Country, and would gain your love' (Act V, sc. 1; p. 336), the conclusion is notably subdued.[6]

Despite these contemporary examples, dramatized early Irish history did not prove especially popular on the stage or in print and it was not until the 1770s that the political moment suggested to other dramatists the possibility of such native subject matter for tragedy. It was in 1773 that Gorges Edmond Howard published *The Siege of Tamor*, a play featuring Turges, King of Denmark, and Malsechlin, King of Leinster, and Monarch of Ireland (Tamor is Howard's ren-

1720), p. 267; further references are included parenthetically in the text.

5 Versions of the story focusing on the abduction of Dervorgilla, wife of Tiernan O'Rourke, by Dermot McMurrough, king of Leinster, which led to the arrival of Strongbow in Ireland, reappear frequently in later Irish writing, including Lady Augusta Gregory's *Dervorgilla* (1907), W.B. Yeats's *Dreaming of the Bones* (1919), and James Joyce's *Finnegans Wake* (1939).

6 For further consideration of these works, see Christopher Wheatley, *'Beneath Iërne's Banners': Irish Protestant Drama of the Restoration and Eighteenth Century* (Notre Dame, IN: University of Notre Dame Press, 2000), pp 41–5, 53–62; Burke, *Riotous Performances*, pp 70–74, 86–87; and Christopher Morash, *A History of Irish Theatre, 1601–2000* (Cambridge: Cambridge University Press, 2002), pp 38–40.

dering of Tara, traditionally regarded as the seat of the high-kings.) In the following year, Francis Dobb published *The Patriot King; or, Irish Chief* (1774), whose hero Ceallachan, the king of Munster, is pitted against Sitrick, chief of the Danes in Ireland.

Later eighteenth-century fiction was even less given to taking episodes from early Irish history as its subject; such an interest in earlier periods of Irish history would have to await the development of the historical novel in the wake of Walter Scott's achievements with Scottish history. Among very few exceptions, Thomas Amory's characteristically eccentric use of Keating's *General History* in *The Life of John Buncle, Esq* (1756, 1766) is most noteworthy.[7]

7 Thomas Amory, *The Life of John Buncle, Esq.* (London, 1756), pp 288–92 (291).

Select bibliography

PRIMARY READING

Butler, Sarah. *Irish Tales*. London: Printed for E. Curll and J. Hooke, 1716.

Keating, Geoffrey (Seathrún Céitinn). *The General History of Ireland*, trans. Dermod O'Connor. London: Printed by J. Bettenham, for B. Crake, 1723.

Walsh, Peter. *A Prospect of the State of Ireland*. London: Printed for Johanna Broom, 1682.

SECONDARY READING

a) Sarah Butler's Irish Tales

Barnard, Toby. *Improving Ireland? Projectors, prophets, and profiteers*. Dublin: Four Courts Press, 2008.

Douglas, Aileen. 'The Eighteenth-Century Novel', in John Wilson Foster (ed.), *Cambridge Companion to the Irish Novel*. Cambridge: Cambridge University Press, 2006. Pp 21–38.

Kilfeather, Siobhán. 'The Profession of Letters, 1700–1810', in *Field Day Anthology of Irish Writing, Vols IV and V: Women's Writing and Traditions*, ed. Angela Bourke and others, 5 vols. Cork: Field Day and Cork University Press in association with Field Day, 2002. Vol. 5. Pp 772–7, 782–7.

King, Kathryn R. *Jane Barker, Exile; A Literary Career, 1675–1725*. Oxford: Clarendon Press, 2000.

Ó Gallchóir, Clíona. 'Foreign Tyrants and Domestic Tyrants: the Public, the Private and Eighteenth-Century Women's Writing', in Patricia Coughlan and Tina O'Toole (eds), *Irish Literature: Feminist Perspectives*. Dublin: Carysfort Press, 2008. Pp 17–38.

Ross, Ian Campbell. '"One of the Principal Nations in Europe": The Representation of Ireland in Sarah Butler's *Irish Tales*', *Eighteenth-Century Fiction*, 7:1 (1994), 1–16.

b) other

Backscheider, Paula R. and Catherine Ingrassia (eds). *A Companion to the Eighteenth-Century English Novel and Culture*. Oxford: Blackwell, 2005.

Baines, Paul and Rogers, Pat. *Edmund Curll, bookseller.* Oxford: Clarendon Press, 2007.

Ballaster, Ros. *Seductive Forms: Women's Amatory Fiction from 1684 to 1740.* Oxford: Clarendon Press, 1992.

Burke, Helen. *Riotous Performances: the struggle for Hegemony in the Irish Theatre, 1712–1784.* Notre Dame IN: University of Notre Dame Press, 2000.

Carnell, Rachel. *Realism, Partisan Politics and the Rise of the British Novel.* Basingstoke: Palgrave Macmillan, 2006.

Cunningham, Bernadette. *The World of Geoffrey Keating: history, myth and religion in seventeenth-century Ireland.* Dublin: Four Courts Press, 2000.

Davis, Lennard J. *Factual Fictions: The Origins of the English Novel.* New York: Columbia University Press, 1983.

Greer, Germaine. 'Women in the Literary Market Place: Pimping in Grub Street', in Sarah Prescott and David E. Shuttleton (eds), *Women and Poetry, 1660–1750.* Basingstoke: Palgrave Macmillan, 2003. Pp 161–79.

Hammond, Brean and Shaun Regan. *Making the Novel: Fiction and Society in Britain, 1660–1789.* Basingstoke: Palgrave, 2006.

Hill, Jacqueline R. 'Popery and Protestantism, Civil and Religious Liberty: The Disputed Lessons of Irish History 1690–1812', *Past and Present* 118 (February 1988), 96–129.

—, 'Politics and the Writing of History: the Impact of the 1690s and 1790s on Irish Historiography', in D. George Boyce, Robert Eccleshall, and Vincent Geoghegan (eds), *Political Discourse in Seventeenth- and Eighteenth-Century Ireland.* Houndmills: Palgrave, 2001. Pp 227–31.

Loveman, Kate. *Reading Fictions, 1660–1740: Deception in English Literary and Political Culture.* Aldershot: Ashgate, 2008.

Hunter, J. Paul. *Before Novels: the Cultural Contexts of Eighteenth-Century Fiction.* New York: Norton, 1990.

MacCarthy, B.G. *The Female Pen: Women Writers and Novelists, 1621–1818.* 1944–7; repr. with an introduction by Janet Todd. Cork: Cork University Press, 1994.

Mac Craith, Mícheál. 'Literature in Irish, *c.*1550–1690', in Margaret Kelleher and Philip O'Leary (eds), *Cambridge History of Irish Literature*, 2 vols. Cambridge: Cambridge University Press, 2006. Vol. I. Pp 191–231.

McKeon, Michael. *The Origins of the English Novel, 1600–1740.* Baltimore and London: Johns Hopkins University Press, 1987.

Morash, Chris. *A History of Irish theatre, 1601–2000.* Cambridge: Cambridge University Press, 2002.

Ó Catháin, Diarmaid. 'Dermot O'Connor, Translator of Keating', *Eighteenth-Century Ireland*, 2 (1987), 67–87.

Ó Ciardha, Éamonn. *Ireland and the Jacobite Cause, 1685–1766: a fatal attachment.* Dublin: Four Courts Press, 2000.

O'Halloran, Clare. *Golden Ages and Barbarous Nations: Antiquarian Debate and*

Cultural Politics in Ireland, c.1750–1800. Cork: Cork University Press in association with Field Day, 2004.

Richetti, John. *The English Novel in History 1700–1780*. London: Routledge, 1999.

Ross, Ian Campbell. 'Fiction to 1800', in Seamus Deane, with Andrew Carpenter and Jonathan Williams (eds.), *Field Day Anthology of Irish Writing*, 3 vols. Derry: Field Day, 1991. Vol. I. Pp 682–759.

—. 'Irish Fiction before the Union', in Jacqueline Belanger (ed.), *The Irish Novel in the Nineteenth Century: Facts and Fictions*. Dublin: Four Courts Press, 2005. Pp 34–51.

—. 'Prose in English 1690–1800: From the Williamite Wars to the Act of Union', in Margaret Kelleher and Philip O'Leary (eds), *Cambridge History of Irish Literature*, 2 vols. Cambridge: Cambridge University Press, 2006, Vol. I. Pp 232–281.

Schellenberg, Betty A. *The Professionalization of Women Writers in Eighteenth-Century Britain*. Cambridge: Cambridge University Press, 2005.

Spencer, Jane. *The Rise of the Woman Novelist: from Aphra Behn to Jane Austen*. Oxford: Blackwell, 1986.

—. *Aphra Behn's Afterlife*. Oxford: Oxford University Press, 2000.

Straus, Ralph. *The Unspeakable Curll; being some of account of Edmund Curll, bookseller; to which is added a full list of his books*. London: Chapman and Hall, 1927.

Todd, Janet. '*The Sign of Angellica*': *Women, Writing, and Fiction, 1660–1800*. London: Virago, 1989.

Wheatley, Christopher J. *'Beneath Iërne's Banners': Irish Protestant Drama of the Restoration and the Eighteenth Century*. Notre Dame IN: University of Notre Dame Press, 2000.

BIBLIOGRAPHY

Loeber, Rolf and Magda Loeber, with Anne Mullin Burnham. *A Guide to Irish Fiction 1650–1800*. Dublin: Four Courts Press, 2006.